THE TERMINATION PROTOCOL

Scott Stiletto Book 1

D1450309

BRIAN DRAKE

WOLFPACK
PUBLISHING
— EST 2013 —

WOLFPACK
PUBLISHING
— EST 2013 —

Published in the United States by Wolfpack Publishing, Las Vegas

Wolfpack Publishing
6032 Wheat Penny Avenue
Las Vegas, NV 89122

wolfpackpublishing.com

Paperback ISBN 978-1-64119-626-0
eBook ISBN 978-1-64119-625-3

THE TERMINATION PROTOCOL

PROLOGUE

Afghanistan – 1987

IT WOULD be a beautiful country, Captain Dimitri Roskov decided, if there weren't snakes with Stinger missiles hiding in the rocks.

Roskov steered the flying tank that was the Mi-24 gunship helicopter through a winding mountain pass, the walls of the canyon on either side sloping to the usual dry terrain common to the whole of Afghanistan. The rocky ledges were potential ambush points where mujahedeen fighters and their US rocket launchers waited. Maybe. Probably.

Roskov sweated beneath his flight suit, his eyes constantly scanning the warning lights to the left of his center instrument panel. They would glow red once the early warning system detected an incoming missile, but Roskov had not survived eighteen missions in the Mi-24 without double- and triple-checking every system his life depended on.

This mission, his nineteenth, couldn't end fast enough.

He flew lead in front of two other Mi-24s spaced out behind him, each carrying more weapons than he. Roskov's chopper only had the 23mm gun pod, and he hadn't bothered to engage the safety on his control stick. Should any mujahedeen present themselves, he needed to open fire and get clear so his escorts could destroy the threat. The payload mounted underneath his helicopter could not fall into American hands should he be shot down. If he was shot down and survived the crash, he had orders to activate the gunship's self-destruct mechanism and kill himself with the 9mm Makarov in a flight suit pocket. With the gunship's armor plating, he'd more than likely survive anything other than a direct hit from a Stinger.

The payload wasn't the usual explosive shell Roskov was used to dropping on enemy camps. The cylindrical steel canister contained a nerve gas nicknamed ZH4 but officially designated zanimicrochloraldite 4004 or z4004. It was a colorless and odorless sarin nerve agent, supercharged by Soviet scientists to kill within thirty seconds. Normal sarin caused death within ten minutes.

And there was a special target for the ZH4, too.

Roskov and his team were heading for the Panwa region. It seemed more arid than elsewhere in the country, but it all looked the same to Roskov. The leadership of the White Leopard Brotherhood, major players in the mujahedeen, were gathering for a strategy session, and Moscow wanted the group violently wiped out—a perfect job for the ZH4.

The weight of the canister had required the subtraction of most other weapons, hence Roskov's escorts.

Roskov swallowed, his throat dry. The valley walls continued flashing by. The warning panel remained quiet, but he knew better than to drop his guard. Ten more minutes to target.

JUBAIR AHMED counted three Mi-24s in his spotting scope and quickly stashed it in a pocket. He hefted the Stinger missile launcher to his shoulder.

He sat in a makeshift snipers' nest behind a cluster of rocks, the canyon's wall swooping downward mere feet from him. The opposite side of the yawning canyon was identical, and it concealed his teammate Ilias. Jubair and Ilias were young fighters barely out of their teens, and already they had numerous Mi-24 kills to their credit. Today they were the vanguard of protection for the Brotherhood meeting.

When the thumping helicopters finally appeared, he let out a curse. There were him and Ilias, their two Stingers, and three gunships. He primed the rocket and sighted through the eyepiece. The only chance they had was to knock out two and hope the third followed what most Soviet pilots did: turn tail once they were alone.

Jubair waited. The gunships flew low, but the Stinger could still get them from the elevated position from which Jubair was firing. The Russians were making the mistake of thinking the Stinger could only fly from surface-to-air.

The viewfinder showed eighty yards. Ilias would not fire until Jubair did. He set the sights on the lead gunship.

The air was hot and dry, the surface beneath him hard and uncomfortable. Tiny rocks poked through Jubair's thin clothing. Jubair endured because otherwise his country would be lost to the Russians. His family had already suffered greatly since the invasion in '79, his father and sister dead, another brother a prisoner of war, and his mother missing. She was probably dead, buried somewhere in an unmarked grave, but until Jubair knew for sure, he chose to believe she was still alive and fighting.

If the Russians said they'd leave after he shot down fifty helicopters, Jubair would shoot down a hundred to make them leave faster. Today he would add at least two more to his total.

Seventy-five yards. Sixty. Jubair mouthed a silent prayer and fired the Stinger.

The shudder of the heavy launcher shook him from head to toe, and the missile left the tube, an angry spout of flame blazing from the rear rocket motor. White smoke trailed the missile. The explosive projectile closed the distance at incredible speed, but Jubair's heart quickly sank.

The lead gunship pulled into a steep climb and raced for the open sky above, ejecting flares to confuse the heat-seeking missile and send it careening into the wall of the valley. The explosion sent clouds of flame and dust into the air.

From across the valley, a second missile fired, zeroing

in on the second gunship as that pilot turned his guns toward Jubair. The rocket smashed into the fuselage and detonated—a direct hit. The gunship split in two, both fiery sections falling to the valley floor.

The third gunship veered in Jubair's direction, following the still-visible smoke trail from his Stinger. Jubair stood to meet his doom, staring through the canopy glass as the gunship neared and the pilot unleashed a stream of rockets. Jubair's world went black before he felt the impact of the salvo.

THE G-FORCES pushed Roskov into the back of his seat as he climbed. Five thousand feet. Seven thousand. His warning lights flashed wildly, the alarm blaring. His countermeasures had defeated the Stinger, but the alarm was still wailing.

That meant there was another missile locking on.

Roskov keyed his radio. "Federov, how many are there? Federov, do you copy?"

Another voice came over the radio. Vasily, the third pilot. "Two targets destroyed. We're clear."

Roskov acknowledged and leveled off, then turned and pointed his nose back toward the canyon, pulling back into a hover. His heart sank when he saw the burning wreckage of Federov's chopper.

"Direct hit, Captain," Vasily told Roskov, his machine circling nearby. "He had no chance."

"Back on course," Roskov ordered, swinging the Mi-24 back in the direction of their target. "They'll pay for this."

Roskov pushed his throttle to full, and the jolt of the acceleration forced him back into the seat once again.

ILIAS ABU-AHMED watched his friend Jubair die in a hail of rockets and flame. The Soviets had claimed another martyr, but he'd make them pay.

He sighted his Stinger and loosed his own projectile in reply, jumping from his prone position and running for the rocks behind him. He heard the explosion and felt the shockwave push against his back. He stole a glance back. The third gunship was now turning his way. Cannons roared behind him. Ilias dropped and rolled into a narrow crevice as the ground exploded around him. He kept the back of his neck covered and made himself small as the strafing continued. Rock chips stung his exposed skin. The huge gunship flashed overhead, and Ilias stayed flat while the gunship spun around and flew over a second time. Agonizing minutes passed as the two surviving choppers hovered before turning to continue on. Ilias looked up only when he heard the engines fading in the distance.

Ignoring the dust and grit covering his clothes and making his face itch, he broke into a sprint, racing for his horse, which was ground-tethered fifty yards away.

Swinging into the saddle, he spurred the horse onward, the animal galloping at full speed. He wouldn't be able to stop the attack on the camp, but maybe he could help once he arrived.

ROSKOV STARTED flicking switches to arm the bomb. His warning lights began flashing once again as the camp radar picked him up, but he stayed focused. Vasily zoomed past him, rockets and cannons blazing, to take out the surface-to-air guns ringing the camp.

Puffs of smoke exploded around him, the flak shells signaling he was in range. The gunship shook with each explosion, but none of the shells burst close enough to damage the helicopter. Even if they did, they were low-power French anti-aircraft shells and nowhere near a match for his armor.

Roskov slowed his breathing. Vasily swooped in low, ground explosions in his wake, and Roskov got his first glimpse of people running for cover around the camp. Soldiers stood and fired at him, but if the ineffectual bullets were bouncing off his underbelly, he couldn't tell.

"Get clear, Vasily," he said into his radio as his left index finger found one more switch and the ZH4 canister fell from its clamp.

The chopper drifted up a hair as the extra weight of the cylinder vanished, and he pulled back into yet another climb. Vasily radioed that he was following. At ten thousand feet, he leveled off, circled back, and tipped the chopper at a downward angle to get a look at his handiwork.

A neat cloud in the center of the camp spiraled upward, the blast having ripped a crater in the earth. Fire and debris were spreading throughout the camp. Tents burned. He couldn't make out figures at this height, but it didn't matter. By the time he and Vasily started on their course back to base two minutes later, everybody on the ground was dead.

ILIAS PULLED his horse up short as soon as he heard the blast.

The horse whinnied and shifted when the shockwave reached them. The thunder followed.

The orange ball of flame dissipated quickly, faster than normal, Ilias thought as he pushed the horse onward at a trot. What remained was a cloud of white smoke. Thick white smoke. It hung in the air since there was no breeze to clear it. When Ilias came over the last rise before the camp's perimeter, he heard the screams.

The camp consisted of tents and wooden buildings. All were obviously damaged, but the inhabitants were either lying still on the ground or thrashing around before their bodies stopped moving altogether. Ilias remained on the rise, his eyes fixed on the horror, his horse breathing hard. Presently the last scream faded, but the white cloud remained. Obviously, the Russians had not dropped an ordinary bomb. They had used a chemical agent of some type, and it was lethal.

No way Ilias was going any closer. He swallowed hard, his throat dry and seemingly choked with dust, and ordered his body off the horse. On shaky legs, his breathing shallow, he found a camera in the left-side saddle bag. One of the Americans who often visited the country had handed him the camera and asked him to bring it back if he ever photographed something worth showing him. He stayed well away, but Ilias began a slow circle of the camp, taking one picture after another. The camera had the ability to zoom in, and Ilias took advantage of the feature. After he finished, he dropped to his knees and vomited into the dirt.

CHAPTER ONE

Central Intelligence Agency – Present Day

GENERAL ISAAC Fleming sat behind his clean desk at CIA headquarters. He had a headache centered right behind his eyes. He was the man in charge of the Special Activities Division, the leader of a staff of "skull smashers" who pulled off the impossible and most dangerous missions. It was his job to have headaches on a regular basis, but the cause of the current painful throb brought more distress than normal.

The report he held in his hand detailed information about a Russian chemical weapon called ZH4, now for sale on the black market. He had thought the nerve gas had long ago been destroyed. An addendum to the report detailed the recent Russian investigation to discover where the canisters had come from, but that provided little solace. The horse had left the stable. He couldn't imagine the catastrophe if the gas fell into the wrong hands—and were there any *good* hands for something like that? The one time the Soviets had used the weapon would be forever etched in his memory, and he'd only seen pictures of the aftermath. He was looking at those pictures from Afghanistan once again. They were attached to the report on the ZH4's potential sale.

He keyed the intercom on his telephone.

"David?"

Fleming's chief of staff and number two, David Mc-Neil, responded from the outer officer without delay. "Yes, sir?"

"Tell Scott I need to see him right away."

"He just got back from Tangiers, sir. He's at home."

"Call him. It's urgent."

"Yes, sir."

Fleming's brow wrinkled in thought. Scott Stiletto was one of his best. Scott could be totally cold when necessary, but if he had a fault, it was his do-gooder streak when he found an underdog in need of a defender. For Fleming, he was the perfect operator, with the proper mix of humanity and ruthlessness.

Fleming returned to his reading. The analysts who had prepared the report not only detailed the sale of the nerve gas, but also the name of the person brokering the deal. The buyer remained a mystery. While he waited, he made calls to arrange Stiletto's transport and backup.

SCOTT STILETTO lay awake in bed.

It had been a rough couple of days since his return from Tangiers, as was always the case after a mission. The Tangiers job hadn't been particularly rough, the objective being to bring back to the US an undercover asset who had been deeply involved in jihadist operations and had critical information for the CIA Stiletto had accomplished the mission, and the undercover asset was now safely tucked away at an Agency safe house where he could be debriefed and his information processed. It might have been routine, but the mental and physical effort required to complete the mission had left him drained.

Yet he couldn't sleep. He didn't want to think about why.

He knew why.

The ringing phone startled him, and he rolled over to grab the cell from the nightstand. Heavy curtains covered his bedroom windows, blocking out most of the sun. A sliver of light looked like a sharp blade across the carpet.

"Yes?" he answered.

"It's David," McNeil said. Fleming's chief of staff.

"What's up?"

"A chemical weapon is loose," McNeil replied. "The boss wants to see you ASAP."

"I just got home. Tell him to go to hell."

"You can tell him yourself when you get here," McNeil said.

Stiletto sighed and gave up. "I wasn't sleeping anyway."

"See you soon."

Stiletto rose, showered and shaved, and pulled on blue jeans and a gray polo. He wouldn't need his pistol for the meeting, so he collected it from where it sat on top of his dresser and secured the weapon in the wall safe contained in his closet.

Stiletto climbed into his car, a 1978 Trans Am that he had restored piece-by-piece, the original black replaced by candy apple red. The car was his second hobby, the first being an incessant habit of sketching, although he never quite finished anything he drew. Always reaching into his imagination for subject matter, he often felt that he was searching for something in his drawings that remained forever elusive. It was as if he were trying to solve a problem he couldn't quite identify, even though he had plenty of problems that were easy to name.

The Trans Am's 454 engine rumbled all the way to CIA headquarters in McLean. Showing his pass at the main gate, he was allowed through and parked near the main entrance.

Stiletto crossed the Agency seal in the main lobby and paused for a moment to glance at the Memorial Wall, where anonymous stars represented the CIA agents who had died in the field. Scott let out a long breath. Sometimes he didn't even notice the memorial was there. He hated to admit it, but the wall blended in with the rest of the scenery. He figured it was that way with everybody else, too. Nobody paid attention until there was a ceremony to honor another anonymous addition, and such ceremonies were so few and far between that some employees retired having never attended one.

Every morning he crossed the seal and passed the wall with his thoughts only on the coffee counter beyond the security gate. But he saw it now, a grim reminder that he could end up on that wall too.

He moved on.

Most Agency employees wore green badges to identify themselves. Contract employees, of whom there were too many in Scott's opinion, wore blue badges. The operatives in Stiletto's division were a different animal. They wore black badges, which allowed them access to the sub-basement offices of the Special Activities Division. Their badge color and department name generated some good jokes through the building, with SAD operatives being called "the Black Death Legion," "the Executioners," and Stiletto's favorite, "the Xanax Squad."

The elevator opened on the sub-basement hallway. Doors lined the hall on both sides, behind which he and his colleagues shared working space. Stiletto headed straight for the door at the end of the hall. General Ike's office.

David McNeil sat behind the outer office desk.

"Go on in."

Stiletto opened the door to Fleming's office.

"SIT DOWN, Scott. We have a big one."

Stiletto eased into the chair in front of the general's desk, his pulse quickening at the general's words. Who needed rest when there was action? The man behind the desk might have been his boss, but they were also good friends, or at least he thought so. Sometimes the general could be a little aloof about his feelings toward the team. Pictures around the office showed General Fleming at various stages of his Army career. He'd only been in charge of SAD for three years, having joined after retiring from the military, but to Scott, it felt like he'd been there forever. Fleming knew how to champion his people, and they wanted to do right by him because he took care of them.

No family pictures adorned the desk. Fleming kept family details private, but everybody knew he'd been married to the same woman for almost forty years. He had sharp blue eyes and dark hair, and a scar on his right cheek. Those blue eyes bored into Stiletto as the interview began.

"ZH4 nerve gas. Ever hear of it?"

"No, sir."

"Developed during the '70s by the Russians, who later destroyed it in the '90s. Allegedly."

Stiletto suppressed a frown. The general always kept his words short when a situation caused one of his migraines. He, on the other hand, wanted to hear more. "Did the Russians ever use it?"

"Once. Afghanistan, 1987. Horrible results."

Fleming opened the folder in front of him and set in front of Stiletto four glossy black-and-white photographs. Stiletto leaned forward to examine them. His stomach turned.

Each picture showed a camp in the desert, the ground littered with bodies, the few visible faces etched with agony.

"ZH4," Fleming said, "is a form of sarin gas the Soviets modified to kill within a minute. Normal sarin takes ten minutes. They used it in this case to kill off leaders of the mujahedeen."

Stiletto sat back, his face neutral but his mind racing. Death and violence were nothing new to him, and he'd contributed his share. Wholesale slaughter, on the other hand, was something he couldn't tolerate. *Wouldn't* tolerate, on US soil, or the soil of any other nation. And as long as he had the power to prevent such tragedies, Stiletto felt it was his duty to do so.

"You said 'allegedly' destroyed, sir?"

"Right. A canister of the gas is up for sale."

"We need to stop that."

"You read my mind. I have a report here from the Russians saying they investigated where the nerve gas came from and traced it to some former soldiers who kept a stash for themselves when the USSR ended their chemical weapon programs. One has been released for sale. The others have been recovered, and the perpetrators dealt with."

"Sounds like the Russians should be doing this job."

"Ideally, but our people discovered the next piece of the puzzle. An arms dealer named Hamid Fasil is selling the canister to an unknown buyer. We have the time and place of the deal. The president wants the ZH4 recovered as a priority, but if there's a chance to take out Fasil and his buyer, that shouldn't be ignored."

Stiletto made a fist. The missions were never easy, but he liked it that way. The chase. The capture.

The kill.

"Just point me in the right direction, sir."

Fleming passed Stiletto a file folder with the words Top Secret emblazoned in red across the center.

"It's all there. Your transportation arrangements have been squared away. Read and destroy."

Stiletto took the folder and rose from the chair. When he was halfway to the door, Fleming called, "Scott?"

He turned.

"Good luck."

Stiletto winked.

CHAPTER TWO

LESS THAN four hours after his meeting with the general, Stiletto crossed the runway at a private CIA airfield in the outskirts of Virginia and stepped aboard a private jet. He carried a large seabag containing his gear.

The jet was a Cessna Mustang with twin engines mounted behind the wings. While the Agency no longer officially operated Air America, the CIA ran its covert transportation efforts through a variety of front companies using an equally wide variety of aircraft, both those available to the civilian and corporate worlds and some custom-built for covert purposes.

The Cessna Mustang had been built with features specifically designed for the Agency. One could not jump out of such a plane because of the risk of being sucked into the engines, so to compensate, a door had been constructed in the belly of the plane that would slide open to allow exit. One might think the government would buy a different plane that would allow a jump via traditional means, but one also never expected the government to run anything efficiently.

The low light did little to conceal the tan carpet and leather seats. It was a far cry from the loud, cramped, and cold C-130 Hercules transports Stiletto had been shuffled around in during his Army days.

He opened the sea bags and started going over his equipment. Draped over the ballistic vest he wore was his load-bearing harness, a pair of suspender-like straps connected to a pistol belt. Two fragmentation grenades were attached to each strap. From the belt hung magazine pouches and the holster for his Colt Combat Government .45 ACP autoloader, an older Series 70 generation pistol rebuilt to his own specifications. The Heckler & Koch UMP sub-machine gun,.45-caliber, completed the ensemble. For the long-range work he expected, he had an M-24 sniper rifle with a night scope chambered in man-killing 7.62mm NATO.

The inspection, including that of the audio surveillance gear, took about an hour. He left his gear spread out on the floor while he sat in one of the leather seats and hoped for sleep. He didn't want to stay awake with the drone of the engine lulling his mind into thoughts he'd rather not have filtering through. The kind that kept him awake.

Stiletto had entered the Army at nineteen to provide for him and a young wife named Maddy who was pregnant with their daughter. He quickly discovered that if Uncle Sam had wanted him to have a family, they'd have issued one, and caring for the child while carrying out his duties presented hardships Stiletto and Maddy hadn't known existed. But they persevered. Stiletto entered Special Forces, serving at various stations all over the world, and then took the option of retirement at the rank of major. Scott wanted to settle in New York, where he could get a private security position and enjoy time with his family.

And then Maddy died.

Stiletto took out his phone to play solitaire. He didn't want to think about any of that right now, but neither Maddy nor his daughter Felicia was ever far from his thoughts, especially because Felicia had refused to speak with him after her mother died. He still didn't know why she was angry with him.

The flight droned on. All Stiletto knew for sure was that he was heading for Iraq, a small corner of that large country, to keep two sides from buying a chemical weapon that could wipe out hundreds within minutes.

He forced his thoughts to the mission.

CHAPTER THREE

"THOSE TWO guys are watching us."

Robert Moray raised an eyebrow and peered at the scruffy face of Darius Porter, who sat to his left.

"I noticed."

"They're locals."

"Probably aren't used to seeing Americans here."

"They're trouble, Bobby."

"We'll deal with it," Moray said. "If we must."

Moray trusted Porter's instincts. Porter was a hardened mercenary, having joined Moray's crew from one of the larger merc companies in Europe. He'd probably forgotten more about warfare than Moray had ever learned, so Moray paid attention.

Moray, Porter, and a redheaded woman named Kylie Sarto sat at a corner table in a small café. Moray and Kylie were an item. The boss had not wanted him bringing her on the mission, but he had refused to go without her, and nobody else in the organization knew this back corner of Iraq as well as Moray so the boss had relented.

Plates of chicken, goat, bread, and various curries for

dipping had been placed at the center of the table, and most of the meal and dips now consumed, except for a few bits and pieces. They drank tea, with a steaming pot near Moray's right arm. They were somewhere in a far corner of Iraq, far from the usual American military presence, and Moray hoped that the attention from the two men across the café was merely curiosity instead of danger.

Kylie Sarto let out a breath. "I think we've covered everything," she suggested. "We should go."

Moray swallowed a piece of chicken. The meat was juicy and tender and spiced just right. He'd been briefing the team on their operation for the evening, the interception of the ZH4 nerve gas.

"Nothing short of victory is acceptable tonight," he told them.

Porter and Kylie nodded.

"If we fail," Moray continued, "assuming we survive, we answer to the top dog. Zolac made that clear. He won't like us if we fail."

"We won't," Porter said. "We have the hardware. But why couldn't we simply buy the nerve gas?"

"Zolac says the seller wanted more than our fearless leader was willing to pay," Moray replied. "You don't become a billionaire by spending all your cash in one place. So, we steal it. After that, we go to the extraction point. A chopper picks us up, and away we go."

"It's never that simple," Porter said.

Moray gave him a hard look this time. He respected Porter's experience, but the man's pessimism had no place at the table.

"Enough," Moray snapped. He drank some tea. "Are we ready?"

Porter and Kylie nodded. It was a needless question. They'd all been ready to leave shortly after the food arrived because the hard wooden chairs made their rear ends sore. Moray rose and stretched. It felt good to stand. He went to the counter to pay while the other two stepped toward the door. Moray glanced at the two men Porter was so concerned about. They weren't watching them anymore, but one was dialing his cell phone.

Maybe Porter was right.

His team was prepared for battle. Each wore a heavy coat, not only against the nighttime cold but to cover weapons. Handguns were acceptable for Moray and Kylie, nine-millimeter Model 92 Berettas. Porter had the real firepower. In a special sling under his coat rested an Uzi machine pistol with a twenty-five-round magazine full of high-velocity stingers. If the locals wanted to cause trouble, they'd meet a fusillade of resistance.

The trio turned left out of the café and followed the sidewalk. The town had paved sidewalks and roads, but enough sand from the surrounding desert blew into the area to create a thin layer on the pavement. Their shoes crunched as they walked to a parking lot between the café and the neighboring building. The lot wasn't very large, with room for only a dozen vehicles at most, and a majority of the slots were empty. Their Range Rover waited ten yards ahead. Porter looked up and down the street, turning to check their backside. Moray and Kylie walked with purpose toward the waiting vehicle. Moray fingered the keys in a pocket.

Kylie said, "Bobby—"

Moray didn't stop. The Beretta 92 under his left arm gave him the comfort he needed.

Two scrawny Iraqis loitered by the Rover. One smoked a foul-smelling cigarette while the other stared at them. Their clothes looked new. Moray, Kylie, and Porter stopped midway to the vehicle.

The smoker exhaled a cloud of smoke and said, "We want the woman."

Moray grunted. Human traffickers. No doubt redheaded Kylie would fetch a great deal of money.

Kylie's response was automatic. She laughed.

Her short red hair gave anybody paying attention a warning about her fiery personality. She was tall and thin, with long toned legs that were as lethal as her pistol. She was a martial arts expert, and Moray had seen her use those legs to great effect.

The non-smoker drew a gun from behind his back. He didn't point the gun at them. He held it almost non-threateningly, as if trying to scare them. "We're taking her."

Moray whipped out the Beretta 92 in a flash, Kylie clawing for her own pistol. The two Iraqis seemed to hesitate for a moment. Victims weren't supposed to be armed. The non-smoker received a bullet through the left eye for his efforts before he could lift his pistol. He left a splatter of bone and blood on the side of the Rover as he fell.

The smoker moved quickly, drawing his gun while running for the cover of the Rover's front end. Two shots from Kylie missed the mark and smacked into the Rover's front quarter panel just above the tire.

Porter called, "Behind us!"

The mercenary pivoted as the rumble of an engine joined the echo of the handguns. He threw back his coat and brought up the Uzi. He fired a full-auto blast on the truck, the muzzle flash filling the dark parking area with a strobe effect. Blood spurted from driver's neck, filling the cabin with red and bits of pink, but the two men jumping out the back—the ones from the café, each of whom cradled an AK-47, so common in these parts. They landed solidly on the concrete and let the Kalashnikovs talk.

Moray and Kylie dived for cover as flame spat from the muzzles of the automatic rifles. Moray expected Porter to do the same, but he didn't move. With his feet firmly planted, he stroked the Uzi's trigger once. One of the men fell, and the blood pooling beneath him mixed with the sand to create reddish gunk on the ground. The other dodged behind the truck, lining up his sights on Porter, but his head was just high enough for Porter to get off a shot first. The Uzi spat flame again, and the man dropped like a puppet with its strings cut.

Kylie screamed.

The smoking Iraqi, his cigarette still dangling from his lips and bobbing up and down as he moved, grabbed Kylie from behind. She struggled, but the man had a powerful grip. Moray jumped into an isosceles stance with the Beretta in both hands, but the man shifted so that Kylie's head covered his face.

Porter shouted, "Let her go!" He had the Uzi tucked into his shoulder and was shifting to find a clear shot.

Kylie let go of her Beretta, the gun clattering on the pavement, and sent a bony elbow into the Iraqi's face. Stunned, his grip relaxed. She broke free, spinning to launch one of those long legs straight up into his chin. The Iraqi's head snapped back. She followed up with a twirl and planted a heel in his midsection. The Iraqi tumbled to the ground, his cigarette finally falling, coming to rest against the skin of his neck. He showed no reaction. Kylie picked up her handgun and shot him in the face.

Moray lowered his gun.

The Rover had some bullet damage in the body panels, but the windows and tires remained intact.

Kylie was already running for the Rover, with Moray on her heels and Porter in the rear. The riddled truck blocked the exit, but that was a minor annoyance. Climbing into the Rover, the trio locked their seatbelts, and Moray fired up the engine. He pulled out and powered around the truck, blasting into the street.

Moray asked if anybody was hurt, and Kylie and Porter said no. The scenery of the town flashed by, and within minutes, they were out on the open road surrounded by flat desert, the headlamps piercing the blanket of darkness ahead.

"This is a lousy way to start the mission," Porter remarked.

"But good shooting," Moray replied. "May we be as lucky tonight."

Moray glanced in the rearview mirror. Not so much at Porter, who was shoving fresh cartridges into the Uzi's magazine, but at the blanket in the back covering the rest of their gear. He smiled. Yeah. The enemy would never know what hit them, and he and his team would be gone before the smoke cleared.

CHAPTER FOUR

"CONTROL TO Boy Scout. Status update."

The voice startled Scott Stiletto. He hadn't communicated with his "guardian angel" in more than an hour, and the voice was welcome. The "angel" in this case sat in a room at an air base somewhere in Nevada and controlled the Predator drone that would provide backup when the fireworks started.

"Boy Scout to Control, in position and freezing. Over."

"Hang in there."

Stiletto sat behind a cluster of rocks on the side of a hill overlooking the target area, which was approximately a hundred yards away. Two trucks sat in a flat and open area of desert. A batch of men armed with automatic weapons roamed around.

The cold bit with ferocity. His body and legs were warm enough, but his arms, feet, and the part of his face not covered by his ski-mask (mouth, nose, eyes) felt the chill. If the directional microphone and recording equipment beside him had contained a built-in heater, it would have been a perfect night under the vast array of stars above. But it wasn't a perfect night. It was cold, and he sat on the hard ground. He'd at least slept on the plane prior to jumping into the desert combat zone.

The microphone, aimed at the general area where the trucks sat, hadn't detected any real chatter since his arrival, only coughs and grunts. The headphones he wore warmed his ears a little.

A gust of wind kicked up debris. Bits of rock and dirt cluttered his hiding space. The Kevlar body armor squeezed his torso but did not make breathing difficult. Some rock bits had wound up down his back, and the small pieces rubbed against his skin every time he moved.

The HK UMP sub-machine gun was slung across his back. Resting on a rock in front of him was the M-24 sniper rifle with the night-vision scope on top of the receiver. Somebody moved in front of the truck, and a brief flash of light indicated the use of a cigarette lighter. Stiletto picked up the rifle and peered through the scope. The man standing in front of the truck looked like Hamid Fasil, the seller of the ZH4 nerve gas. Thin, medium height, close-cropped hair. He inhaled sharply on the cigarette and exhaled a cloud of smoke. Another man joined him. The second man cradled an automatic rifle. Fasil did not appear to be armed.

"They're late," the second man said, his voice loud and clear through the headphones.

"Relax," Fasil told him. "We'll give them a little more time."

The second man grunted and remained near Fasil, who appeared not to notice him any longer as he smoked.

Stiletto scooted back from the scope to blink a few times. The green glow of the night vision irritated him after prolonged exposure. He looked at the truck with his naked eyes for a while.

Then Fasil said, "Here they come."

The man with the automatic rifle whistled and the other troops snapped to attention, fanning out around the second truck. That was where the ZH4 would be.

Scott radioed Control to zero in on the first truck. If possible, he didn't want the second one damaged.

"Copy," Control said. "Be advised we see two trucks heading your way. One is running without lights and is approaching from the south."

"What's the direction of the other truck?"

"East."

Stiletto acknowledged and frowned. Were the buyers coming in two separate vehicles, or was the third vehicle the buyers' security team?

Stiletto picked up the M-24 and cycled the action to chamber the first round.

Four minutes ticked by. The buyers finally reached Fasil, their truck trailing a cloud of dust. The buyers parked with their headlights blazing on Fasil's truck. Fasil waved, then flicked away his cigarette. As the buyers emerged, Stiletto put the night scope on them. Four men, three armed. The leader approached Fasil and they shook hands, exchanging greetings. The buyer had an accent Stiletto couldn't place. He focused the scope on the man's face, noting its smooth lines and the man's large nose. The face rang no bells in Stiletto's mental mug file.

"Control?"

"Got both parties."

"Where's the other truck?"

"I took eyes away to watch the buyers, so I'm not sure now."

"Stay focused where you're at," Stiletto said. "When I give the signal, light 'em up."

"Copy."

The missing vehicle nagged the back of Stiletto's mind. He touched the M-24's trigger.

Fasil and the buyer traded jokes about their security, but the chat was short-lived as the buyer called for an assistant, who slung his rifle to bring forward a briefcase. He placed the case on the hood of Fasil's truck, opening the lid to show the payment. Fasil counted some of the money and closed the case. He snapped his own orders, and two men went to the back of the second truck to retrieve a large cylinder. Stiletto focused his scope on the cylinder. About as tall as a wine barrel but thinner, with two handles on either side. The men carrying it grunted with effort as they placed the cylinder on the ground in front of Fasil's truck.

"As agreed," Hamid Fasil said.

The buyer and his man reached for the cylinder.

"Control, change target to the second truck; repeat, second truck. Nerve gas is at the first truck and I don't want to blow it up."

"Copy, Boy Scout."

Stiletto settled his sights on Fasil's forehead and tightened on the trigger.

The buyer suddenly stiffened, a splash of blood striking Fasil and his truck. Fasil reacted with a shout. The echo of a shot followed, a sharp crack that stretched across the desert.

But Stiletto hadn't fired.

"Control, find that other truck. It's an ambush."

"Copy."

The security teams fanned out, Fasil shouting orders at his men as more automatic weapons fire crackled from somewhere nearby. Stiletto swung the M-24 left and right, finding no sign of the shooters. His position did not allow him a full view of the area.

He listened to the gunfire. Heavy thumps. One machine gun, but the string of fire poured non-stop—a belt-fed weapon. The security teams fired back, the gunfire louder now, but none seemed to know who they were shooting at or where to aim. They fired in all directions.

Stiletto cursed. What was going on down there?

The shooting stopped for a moment, the echo fading, and Fasil shouted more orders. The buyers turned their guns on Fasil's crew, one of them accusing Fasil of a setup and Fasil loudly denying the charge.

Then the rocket hit.

Stiletto heard the familiar hiss and whine of the Soviet-era RPG as the rocket-propelled grenade zoomed in, striking the buyer's vehicle. The explosion lit the night. The orange fireball climbed skyward, black smoke coming from the shell of the former vehicle. Fasil and his team fell as the shockwave of the blast hit them, and then a second rocket smacked into Fasil's truck, blowing it to smithereens. Those not killed in the first blast died in the second. Bodies lay scattered like so many Legos.

"Control, tell me you got that other truck."

"Copy, Boy Scout. We have three individuals moving in on foot carrying small arms."

"Copy," Stiletto replied. He scanned the site with his sniper scope. Bodies remained still. Nobody moved. The ZH4 cylinder lay on its side in front of Fasil's burning truck, apparently undamaged. Stiletto focused on that. If he now had only three people to deal with, it made the job easier.

But who were they?

CHAPTER FIVE

MORAY AND his team set up thirty yards from the meeting site.

Porter lay prone behind a sniper rifle while Moray locked a belt of ammunition into an American M-60 machine gun. Kylie held the RPG launcher.

Moray gave the order as the exchange took place. Porter fired first. One man down. As the rest reacted, he opened up with the M-60, the stock hammering against his shoulder as he spread a pattern of rounds at both trucks. Hot brass ejected from the machine gun, but he couldn't hear the tinkle of it hitting the ground over the roar from the muzzle. The hard earth on which he lay was uncomfortable, his jacket not quite heavy enough for the cold, but the rush of adrenaline kept him from thinking about those things as he panned the sights left and right. Return fire didn't bother him. None of the bullets struck anywhere near them. Neither Fasil's men nor the buyers had any idea where to focus their response.

The ammo belt ran dry, the M-60 ceasing fire as if somebody had turned off a switch, and Moray swung his left arm to smack Kylie on her backside. She fired the RPG, the smoke from the rocket lingering as the projectile closed the distance. She quickly fed a second rocket into the launch tube as the first truck exploded and fired again. Second truck gone.

The trio rose, Moray handing Kylie a sub-machine gun from their pile as Porter racked the action on his Uzi. They spread out in a staggered formation and ran to the flaming vehicles.

The desert chill didn't keep sweat from trickling down Moray's back as he led the way, the flames from the two trucks creating a wall of heat they had to pass through to reach the spot where the ZH4 cylinder lay. He hoped it wasn't damaged, but took solace that the heavy stainless-steel construction could take a beating. The release valve on top of the cylinder? That he wasn't sure of. If that had broken, the three of them would be dead before they even touched the thing.

Moray and Kylie broke off to check bodies. Nobody needed a second shot. Kylie signaled the same. Moray turned around. Porter had his sub-machine gun slung and was lifting the ZH4 cylinder upright. All was well or he'd be choking on his own vomit.

Moray approached carefully, nonetheless. "Is it OK?"

Porter examined the container and the release valve and raised a thumb.

Then his head popped like a water balloon. The crack of the shot followed as his body collapsed beside the ZH4.

"Kylie, down!" Moray shouted, hitting the ground hard. Another shot kicked up sand inches from him. He aimed for the hills and let off a burst, and Kylie followed suit. She kept firing as he scooted backward, rose, and ran to her. Another shot struck the ground behind him. Moray reached Kylie and shouted for her to run for the cover of the buyer's burning vehicle. He swept the hillside with a long burst as she moved. When his weapon clicked empty, he pivoted on a heel to follow her.

He should have figured they wouldn't be the only ones who wanted the ZH4.

STILETTO FELT the stock hit his shoulder as the M-24 recoiled.

The man lifting the cylinder of ZH4 nerve gas never knew what hit him as the .308 boat-tail slug separated one side of his head from the other, leaving a bloody mist in the air as he fell.

Stiletto shifted to the other man, zeroing the night scope. The man returned fire, and shots peppered the rocks around Scott. He fired again but missed. He dropped for cover as the return fire continued. When it stopped, he rose again, sighted, and fired as the man ran away. Another miss. A second shooter opened up, and Stiletto highlighted the person in the scope. A woman. He started to squeeze the trigger again when she ran, taking cover behind the flaming wreckage of the buyer's truck. The other man fired again, his shots going wider this time, before he joined her.

Stiletto let out a breath and waited. They had a stalemate. He had the ZH4 covered; they couldn't get to it without exposing themselves.

So much for an easy job. He had planned to let the drone strike do most of the work, walk over to collect the ZH4, and call for his extraction chopper.

Flames continued eating at the vehicles, metal snapping, the putrid scent of burning tires palpable even at his distance. Stiletto tapped the M-24's trigger. It was going to be a long wait. The best way to handle this might just be to work his way down and engage them close up.

"Boy Scout to Control," he said.

"Go ahead."

"What do you see?"

"We have two hostiles using the truck on your left for cover. They're about twenty yards from the vehicle. They aren't moving yet."

"Have you found their vehicle?"

"Negative. We've been keeping our eyes on the action."

"Fly a circuit and see if you can find it. I'm going down there."

"Good hunting."

Stiletto acknowledged and tore off the headset. Checking the HK UMP and his pistol, and plugging a portable com unit into his right ear, he retreated through the narrow path behind him. He stepped carefully so he didn't slip and presently gained the flat ground again. Breaking into a sprint, he rounded the hill, and the burning vehicles came into view. Stiletto advanced at a trot, the UMP at his shoulder, the muzzle probing ahead.

MORAY SAID, "We can't just sit here."

They were far enough from the flaming truck to not get burned, but the wave of heat was impossible to avoid, making them both sweat. Breathing was tough, and Moray's eyes itched from the smoke.

"I'm open to suggestions, lover," Kylie said.

"Can you make it back to the Rover?"

"For what?"

"The RPG, for one. And the Rover itself."

"Are you sure they aren't coming for us?"

"I'm not sure of anything right now."

"Okay." She checked her weapon and moved out, circling wide around the burning truck. Moray followed a little behind her, his finger on the trigger of his own weapon and ready to cover her should the unknown enemy appear. There was nothing but pitch-black ahead as she cleared the fire and broke into a sprint for their starting position.

The hill was the best place for the enemy to hide. Moray snapped his sights in that direction. *There! Somebody moving!* He squeezed the trigger.

STILETTO HIT the ground and rolled as slugs whistled through the air. He came up prone, answering with the

HK. One short burst. Movement off to the side—somebody running. Stiletto sighted as another burst came his way, the sand around him kicking up in short geysers. He rolled to his right. Another salvo of return fire. He shifted to see if the runner was still in sight but saw nothing.

Stiletto jumped to his feet and ran forward, turning diagonally to reach the spot where the ZH4 cylinder lay. He fired from the hip to keep the opposition pinned down. The HK was running dry, so Stiletto let the empty magazine clatter to the ground as he reloaded on the run. He gasped as the bright flames and thick smoke affected his view of the battlefield. How do you fight an enemy you cannot see?

Stiletto charged ahead.

A SOLUTION stared Moray in the face.

He ran to one of the fallen troopers, kicking away the man's rifle to search his web gear, and plucked two grenades from the man's harness. One he stuffed in a pocket. Slinging his sub-machine gun, he pulled the pin on the other, holding the explosive orb tightly. The smoke from the burning vehicles was thicker now. He blinked a few times. If the smoke was affecting him, his enemy was suffering the same way. Moray started forward, looking for the enemy. He wondered where Kylie was. Had she been intercepted?

STILETTO COUGHED as he sucked in smoke. He ran past Fasil's burning truck and reached the still-undamaged second truck Fasil's crew had brought. He dropped near the rear wheel close to the tailgate and wiped his eyes. Scooting on his knees to the opposite side, he sighted down the length of the HK and looked for a target.

Nothing.

Back to the other side. The stainless-steel ZH4 cylinder gleamed in the light of the fires. He waited, then a man materialized in the smoke. He wasn't holding a weapon, but a grenade. Stiletto cursed as he fired once and missed. The man pivoted in his direction and tossed the grenade.

Stiletto dropped farther behind the truck, and the grenade landed off to the left. He reached the passenger side as the grenade exploded, feeling the heat of the blast on his back and bits of shrapnel tugging at his clothes. He raised the HK as the man appeared ahead once again and threw another grenade. The explosive arched toward Scott, getting larger as it neared. Stiletto put his feet under him and bolted forward, charging at the man.

The blast behind him lifted him off his feet, carrying him forward a little before he dropped hard on the desert ground. Something slammed into his backside and he screamed, more startled than hurt, the Kevlar blocking the debris from tearing open his skin. His breath left him. As he fired blindly into the thick smoke, the HK clicked empty. He let the UMP fall and drew his Colt pistol. He shifted left, then right, but saw no sign of his quarry.

Stiletto moved left toward where the ZH4 lay, sweeping his pistol back and forth as he moved.

A pair of headlights and a racing engine pierced the smoke. Stiletto raised his gun. Two shots smacked the ground in front of him, and another whistled past his head. Stiletto dropped and rolled. More gunfire. Stiletto kept rolling, stopping as the heat of the burning truck only yards away touched the back of his neck.

He lifted his head. Two figures had the ZH4 by the handles and were carrying it away. They reached the Rover and pushed the cylinder into the back seat. The woman jumped behind the wheel. Stiletto rose and charged forward, only to stop short as the man swung the RPG to his shoulder and let the rocket fly. The motor of the RPG hissed.

Stiletto reversed and broke into a sprint, heading for the second burning truck as the RPG impacted the remains of the first. The angry blast lit the night once again, and pieces of flaming debris rained down. Stiletto shoulder-rolled into the ground and kept rolling away. He stopped on his belly. The dust cloud behind the Rover was his only indication of where the vehicle was. The Colt bucked and roared twice, but the vehicle kept going.

Stiletto coughed and spat, his eyes burning. He keyed his com unit.

"Control!" He coughed.

"Got the Rover in sight."

"Don't fire," Stiletto said. "The nerve gas is on board."

"Tracking," Control replied.

Stiletto retrieved the HK UMP from where he'd dropped it. Reaching into the front pocket of his combat vest, Stiletto withdrew a small digital camera. They needed leads, and no mistake. He ran to the man he had shot. Only part of his face remained, but Stiletto took a picture anyway. Then he saw the tattoo on the man's neck. He set the camera down to tear open the man's shirt, then held the camera close and snapped a shot.

Stiletto looked around, fighting back a coughing fit. He had to pursue the Rover. Fasil's second truck looked okay. He ran to it, pulling open the driver's door. The keys were in the ignition. Would the engine start? He twisted, and the motor roared to life. Stiletto pulled the door shut, put it in Drive, and stomped the gas pedal.

CHAPTER SIX

"I THOUGHT you were a goner, baby," Moray said.

"Never!" Kylie Sarto kept her hands tight on the wheel as the Rover bounced over the rough terrain.

Moray was on his knees in the back seat, the ZH4 cylinder beside him. He faced the back window, trying to spot any signs of pursuit through the dust cloud behind them. He didn't think they had shaken the enemy that easily.

"Was there only the one?" Kylie said.

"Apparently," Moray replied as a thought crept into his head. He powered down the window nearest and stuck his head out, looking up at the sky. If the enemy was American, they had to have a drone overhead. The plan couldn't have been for one man to hijack the ZH4. A missile strike made much more sense. The Rover's engine and the rush of wind were all he heard. No jet motor penetrated. The only thing in the sky was a mass of stars—and then the star pattern was broken by the outline of wings.

"Drone overhead!" he shouted to Kylie.

"They're going to track us to the extraction!"

"Not much we can do about it right now, babe."

Moray sat back and reloaded his sub-machine gun. Too bad about Porter. Sucker never had a chance. He slapped in the magazine with a grimace. He'd avenge the mercenary. Add it to the account owed him by the Americans.

They owed him big.

STILETTO STIFLED a painful grunt as the truck traveled along the desert floor. His left leg hurt, part of his fatigue pants sticking to his calf. He had shrapnel from one of the grenades in his skin for sure.

But there were bigger problems to deal with first. He could live with the pain.

"Control," he said.

"The Rover is about a hundred yards ahead. Can't tell what their destination might be. Recommend we launch, Boy Scout."

Stiletto didn't respond. He thought of the reasons Control was right. They were out in the middle of nowhere. He had ample transportation to take him away from the death zone created by the ZH4. The opposition would be taken out, the nerve gas destroyed, and Stiletto could get to work tracking who these people were via the dead man's tattoo.

"Control, copy and agree. Take out that truck."

"Copy."

Stiletto slowed his vehicle to a stop but didn't turn

around right away. He let the engine idle. He wanted confirmation of the truck's destruction before he got out of there.

THE PREDATOR drone followed the Range Rover very easily. There was nowhere for the Rover to go in the vast open terrain, nowhere to hide from the Predator's night vision camera, which transmitted a clear picture back to Control.

The General Atomics MQ-1 Predator was a sleek, small aircraft that looked like something a large-scale model builder might assemble in his garage. The fire-power it packed made even the biggest skeptic a believer in its capabilities.

Missile pylons under each wing contained one Hellfire missile, an air-to-surface weapon with a high-explosive anti-tank warhead, which was more than enough explosive power for the Rover.

The long-winged Predator with its bulbous front end tipped downward and the rocket motor shrieked as the craft picked up speed.

The Hellfires flashed brilliantly from the pylons under the wing, the twin missiles trailing white smoke as they closed on the target.

THE ORANGE flash of fire from the missiles shone brightly against the starry sky.

Moray never took his eyes off the outline of the drone

above, and as the rockets zeroed in at a rapid rate, he shouted for Kylie to stand by for a sharp left or right turn. He'd have to guess absolutely right. There would be no room for error. The contrails gave the missiles away, and he watched the cloud of exhaust grow ever closer.

At the last second before impact, he shouted, "Right! Now!"

Kylie wrenched the Rover's steering wheel and the SUV veered to the right, hitting some uneven ground and jolting violently. It wasn't as bad as the push that followed the impact of two Hellfire missiles on the spot they had just been, one, then the other, rocking the ground and sending a shockwave in all directions. Kylie fought the wheel as the Rover tipped one way, then the other, Moray staying on the passenger side to keep some weight there so the vehicle didn't tip. When all four wheels finally grabbed the desert floor again, with only the residual cloud from the blasts behind them, Moray let out a breath.

He knew the drones only carried two missiles.

"Stay off-road?" Kylie said.

"For now. Go to the right, and we'll get back on track for the rendezvous."

"CONTROL TO Boy Scout."

"Tell me some good news."

"Negative, sir. We missed."

"Try again."

"We're out of quarters, sir."

Stiletto pounded on the dashboard and pressed on the gas.

"Tell me where they're going."

"Southeast."

"Any other aircraft in the area?"

"Radar shows none."

Stiletto drove on.

After a few minutes, Control came back over the com.

"They're stopping about two miles ahead of you. We now have a chopper on the radar, closing fast."

"Copy," Stiletto said.

He was getting all he could out of the truck considering the terrain, the bumpy ride wearing on him and the wound in his leg, but he fought back the pain and continued driving. He had to stop them.

Stiletto watched the odometer, and as soon as a mile and a half clicked by, he flipped on the headlamps. Straight ahead was the opposition's Rover. Stiletto stomped the brakes. Incoming gunfire was already smacking into the truck. Stiletto slid out the door, low-crawling around to the side with the H&K UMP in hand. He returned fire, aiming as carefully as he could for the areas around the brief muzzle flashes of the enemy. Glass shattered, and bullets hammered metal.

The chopper swooped in low and fast. The side door was open, and a man leaned out on a side-mounted minigun. Stiletto cursed and took cover behind his truck as the cannon flashed fire. Every piece of glass on the truck shattered, the front tires exploding as the hot slugs punctured the rubber, the body groaning on worn shocks as it sank forward.

Stiletto covered the back of his neck and his eyes. The burst was brief but incredibly destructive, shots that hadn't hit the truck striking the ground instead. Choking desert dust filled the air. Stiletto coughed.

He gritted his teeth and swung around the truck with the UMP, only to see the chopper lifting off and flying away.

Stiletto coughed some more. He tried waving away the dust, but that seemed to only create more.

"Control!" *Cough. Cough.* "Control!"

"We're tracking the chopper, but I can't promise we'll be able to stay with it for long."

"Copy. Redirect my extraction to this location. My transportation just got destroyed."

"Messaging now."

Stiletto pulled the com unit off his head and stood, throwing the HK on the ground in disgust. He leaned against the remains of the truck and tried not to choke on the floating dust.

THE PAVE Low stayed a thousand feet above the ocean.

There was no sense of movement as Stiletto looked out the window. The ocean below appeared flat black. Only the stars in the night sky separated the two. Otherwise, the outside environment might have looked like deep space.

When the helicopter touched down on the rear deck of the USS *Bataan*, Stiletto unstrapped from the wall seat and took his time as he exited. He hurt all over. The cold ocean wind screamed across the deck, the complete opposite of the desert stillness. Stiletto clamped his mouth shut to keep his teeth from chattering and crossed the hard steel deck to the hatch leading below. The masthead light flashed against the night sky, and the larger radar antenna and smaller air-warning radar spun in their endless rotations. He'd joined the Army because he hated swimming and being on a boat made him seasick, but the job sometimes required him to go on the water, so on the water, he went. Whether he liked it didn't matter; the mission mattered more.

Following a set of steps to the narrow passageway, banging his elbow on a wall, he squeezed by passing sailors who paid no attention to him. Their assignment to the *Bataan* meant they saw all types of "special guests" who didn't fit normal navy spec. He stopped by the medical unit to have the shrapnel pulled from his leg and the wound cleaned, stitched, and patched. He had various other cuts and bruises, but nothing a shower and a few beers wouldn't fix. The ship's doctor handed him some painkillers should he need them.

Stiletto went to the small cabin he'd been assigned, locked the door, and fell onto a cot. He groaned and rolled onto his side. He had a sea bag of clean clothes waiting in a corner, but that could wait. He didn't bother to turn out the exposed light bulb hanging from the ceiling. Through the walls, the ship groaned and something clanked, normal ship sounds he'd heard a hundred times before on other boats during his career. He quickly dozed off.

AFTER A shower in a too-small bathroom the next morning, where it was almost impossible to move and he kept bashing his elbows, Stiletto visited the ship's doctor to have his bandage changed, then wandered to the crowded galley for breakfast. Scrambled eggs, toast, and a double portion of crispy bacon. He sat at a corner table alone and tried not to dwell on the lifeless steel walls surrounding him. He took a deep breath. It was the job. It was only temporary. Stay focused. The other sailors, who ate and talked loudly, didn't seem to mind, but the sooner he could get back on solid land, the better.

The ship provided Stiletto with a private office, where he had access to a small workspace and computer. The office was another cramped room with secure communications for "special guests." Stiletto felt less and less special by the minute. He clicked the Skype icon and waited.

The screen flickered and the general appeared.

"How's your head, sir?"

"I've had my quota of aspirin for the day. How's it going?"

"Not good, sir. A third party ruined what should have been a simple job." Stiletto gave his boss an update, ending with, "Who else wanted the ZH4 and maybe didn't win the auction?"

"I'll have to check," Fleming said. He made no comment on the circumstances. Some things couldn't be helped. It wasn't Stiletto's fault, but Scott knew the general would ask if he'd found some kind of clue to the opposition's whereabouts.

"Did you find anything that might lead us to the third party?" the general said.

"I did indeed." Stiletto plugged his digital camera into the computer and uploaded the pictures he'd taken of the dead man's tattoo. "I'm sorry I couldn't get the face, but perhaps the tattoo will lead us somewhere."

"We'll get on it," Fleming told him. "Anything else?"

"No, sir."

"How long until you get back?"

"About four days."

"You're going to go bonkers."

"I have plenty of seasick pills, General," Stiletto said.

STILETTO RETURNED to his cabin.

From his personal items in the sea bag, he took an iPad and a sketchbook. He called up his music library, and hard rock, the volume low, played from the tablet. Sitting up on his cot, he opened the sketchbook. His father, a career army officer, had taken his family all over the world, and it had been tough for Scott to make friends while growing up. To take his mind off being alone so much, he'd learned to draw, a sketchbook as constant a companion as his book bag in school, and his pistol as an adult. His current project was a half-finished forest. With a fresh pencil, he started drawing more of it. He drew hurriedly, as if he needed to finish. As if the forest held the answer to a question he hadn't yet been able to articulate.

CHAPTER SEVEN

HEINRICH ZOLAC steered the bright red sports car around a tight corner and pressed the gas, then cursed and stomped the brakes to avoid crashing into a slow-moving minivan. He wove around the van, the engine responding with a low grumble. The wind skimmed over the windshield and brushed his short but spiky hair. He felt the heat of the sun on the top of his head, the close haircut exposing enough of his scalp that he often risked a burn, but he had too much fun driving with the top down to care. He wore a custom-fitted blue Savile Row suit and aviator shades. Flash and dash.

He downshifted to get more grunt from the motor for the last straightaway, then slowed and turned the low-slung roadster into the gated driveway of a steel-and-glass skyscraper. The young guard at the gate waved him through and Zolac powered into the underground garage, where he swung into his reserved parking slot. The two empty slots next to his car were also reserved—for him. Nobody would be scratching his baby.

A short elevator ride brought him to the main lobby,

bright sunlight blasting through the glass front. Two security guards behind a desk rose and greeted Zolac as the man in the suit headed for the elevators.

Near the elevators stood the third guard; an older man, his blue blazer buttoned and ID badge pinned straight. He said, "Good afternoon, sir," as Zolac pressed the call button.

"Mr. Reed, you should be sitting at the desk."

The older man smiled. "If you don't use it, you lose it."

"Indeed."

The elevator opened and Zolac stepped in. The doors slid shut.

Zolac rode up to the twentieth floor where the boardroom was located.

He left the elevator and surveyed the high-ceilinged boardroom, bright from the forward window which took the place of a wall. The twelve men seated around the oval table ceased their chatter as Zolac crossed the room and sat at the head of the table, his back to the glass. The bright light obscured his features, but all twelve men were familiar with his playboy lifestyle and acne-scarred face. He hadn't always been rich.

Zolac said, "Thank you for being here." He scanned the faces, all of which were turned his way. Astute members of the public would recognize some of the twelve from various industrial and corporate enterprises. The rest were unknown because of their criminal endeavors. To Zolac, it was a good mix of minds for the New World

Revolutionary Front, of which he proudly served as second in command while their leader remained safely out of harm's way.

As a writer for leftist newspapers in Europe in his twenties, Zolac had seen life from top to bottom and formed opinions about how governments should respond to their communities. He had also decided that the citizenry were far too slothful and irresponsible to self-govern in any form. His writing attracted the attention of the leader, who looked at him as a kindred spirit, and together, they had built the organization.

Zolac and the leader envisioned a planet where the world's citizens answered to one leader: a benevolent dictator who would do for them what they could not or refused to do for themselves.

By force, if necessary.

Such efforts took money. Agents needed a budget, and operations needed financing. The collective minds involved in the NWRF were masters of subterfuge. Before bringing up the main topic of the meeting, Zolac wanted to know about recent efforts and how much cash they'd brought to the organization.

"Let's talk about the latest doings. Mr. Grunberg?"

A bald man midway down the left side, his round belly partially concealed by the table, consulted notes in front of him.

"The Baden-Solitron merger is not yet resolved, but negotiations continue on both sides."

"What's holding things up? Did the US representatives not raise their offer?"

"They did, but Baden's owner is reluctant to merge despite the benefits."

"Are we persuading him?"

"We have pictures of him with a woman who is not his wife. He will do whatever it takes to keep those pictures hidden. The merger should yield a dividend of ten million dollars."

"Good," Zolac said. "Mr. Frye?"

Another man, with pasty-white skin and wire-framed specs, said, "Our sabotage of the Alaskan oil pipeline resulted in a longer delay than we expected. The pipeline will be down for six weeks, and crude oil prices should rise beyond our prediction as a result."

"Estimated dividend?" Zolac asked.

"Four million dollars."

"Not bad for six weeks' work," Zolac said. "Good, Mr. Frye." He cleared his throat. "Now we talk about our most ambitious project yet, and it is already well underway. Much must remain secret for now, but I can tell you the new project concerns a chemical weapon strike that will be the beginning of uncontrollable chaos in the United States. US voters recently elected a right-wing president, and he is undermining every effort we made during the last administration to topple the US via economic sabotage and pitting the citizens against each other over racial and class divisions. We are now going to accelerate the removal of the new administration and the insertion of our hand-picked candidate. Mr. Bell, the latest, please?"

A stocky man near Zolac's chair, a European free-lance terrorist named Arnold Bell, said, "I met personally with Mr. Mustafa in North Africa, and he is providing several squads of his best-trained guerillas, who will find their way into the United States and carry out the orders you gave them."

Zolac nodded. "And the ZH4?"

"Successfully acquired after some difficulty," Bell said, outlining the report given to him by Moray earlier that morning. "Moray and Sarto are in Barcelona now waiting for their next instructions, but the loss of Porter creates problems."

Zolac frowned. "Was it the Americans who tried to stop the sale?"

"The use of the drone would suggest that, yes. And Porter, sir?"

Zolac held up a hand. "Don't worry. I'll go see them in Barcelona myself, and take over for Porter when the time comes."

"But—"

"What we don't have time for," Zolac said, "is getting another operative up to speed."

Bell nodded.

Zolac knew there would be complications going into the operation. Worse, the dead operative, Porter, might be traced back to them. But there was nothing to do but go forward and meet future challenges as they arrived. They had worked too hard to cut and run.

Zolac smiled at the faces before him. He would have a good conversation with their leader in an hour when he updated the man on their progress. Zolac ended the meeting without taking questions and dismissed the gathering, but remained seated. He asked Bell and Frye to remain. Arnold Bell stayed in his seat. As Frye sat down once again, his hands started to shake.

The others, talking amongst themselves, cleared the room. Zolac smiled. The smile did not brighten his gray eyes.

"Stand up, Mr. Frye."

The man with the wire-framed specs, sweat now covering his pale skin, stood. A blond man in black with a barrel torso entered the conference room and stopped at the table. Bell and Zolac watched the new arrival. Frye did not. Frye's eyes stayed on Zolac.

"Mr. Frye," Zolac said, "I don't mind you making money on the side, but I do mind when you do it by selling me out."

"But—"

The rest of Frye's words stopped in his throat as the barrel-chested man snapped a wire garrote around the pale man's neck and pulled tight. Frye gurgled and struggled, and the big man grunted with effort and pulled tighter. Presently Frye's body slackened with one last choked rattle.

"Remove him," Zolac said.

The big man hoisted Frye over his shoulders and carried him out of the room.

Bell said, "What did he do?"

"He was planning to steal the ZH4 and sell it on his own," Zolac said.

"I hope we don't have too many similar complications, Heinrich."

"We won't. All we have to do now is remain patient."

Zolac rose and smoothed the front of his suit. "Let's go to my office. I could use a drink."

GENERAL IKE called McNeil into his office. While he waited, he swallowed an aspirin with some water. Stiletto's news had set his usual headache to full throttle.

The door opened, and McNeil entered and sat down without being told. A covert ops veteran, he'd only taken the chief-of-staff job after losing his left leg during an assignment. He walked so well with a prosthetic limb that nobody could tell he had no leg from the knee down unless he wore shorts.

General Ike began, "We have a problem," and told him about the outcome of Stiletto's mission.

"Our intel didn't indicate there were other players who wanted the ZH4," McNeil said.

"Either we missed something, or this third party thought they could take advantage. We need to catch up, and fast."

"Did Scott get anything we can use?"

"A picture of a dead man's tattoo. It's slim, but if we can identify the man that tattoo belongs to, we might have some place to start. He emailed it to me, and I forwarded it to you. Expedite the processing."

"Of course, sir. And there's something else. If you hadn't called me, I'd have come in anyway."

Fleming blinked while he waited.

"You might want to pop another aspirin, sir."

"That bad?"

"There's a reporter sniffing around Washington asking about American contractors in Saudi Arabia who are working for us," the chief of staff said. "She's suggesting that these contractors are torturing terrorist suspects."

"We don't torture terrorists," Fleming stated. "Who is this person?"

"Sofia McKay."

"Who does she work for?"

"She's freelance."

"Never heard of her."

"Neither has anybody else," McNeil replied.

"We'll deal with her when the time comes," Fleming said. "Get to work on that tattoo."

McNeil rose from the chair. "Yes, sir," he said, leaving the office.

Fleming sank back in his chair and tapped his upper lip. Turning to the PC on his desk, he typed Sofia

McKay's name into a search box and scrolled through the information that appeared.

She was indeed a freelancer and had a large presence on the internet with her own "news" website, mostly covering organizations dedicated to protesting against the US government and advocating for various left-wing causes. There were videos on her site at such rallies, and Fleming watched a few. She had a camera and a microphone and wasn't afraid to use either, allowing the protestors to air their grievances, whatever they were, but not really covering any hard news. Was prowling DC trying to stir up trouble part of a goal to branch out?

Every now and then a news outlet would run a story on the CIA torturing terrorists, and then there would be an audit of operations, and usually a finger wag or two if "interrogations" stepped beyond legal bounds. The public was convinced that the interrogations depicted on television and in movies were the real deal, but they weren't. Real enhanced interrogation was fairly mild, used to scare a captive rather than harm them. A hurt or dead prisoner was no good for providing information.

But a reporter with an agenda could spin the story in such a way as to create enough fuss to make it difficult to focus on the job at hand. Fleming had enough on his plate with the search for the ZH4. He didn't need Agency auditors and investigators going through his files, threatening his funding, and putting agents at risk.

Because he was in charge of the contractors in Saudi

Arabia, and he knew what they were doing to get the intelligence they required. If any of those contractors stepped out of line even for a moment, he'd have to answer for it. Most of those contractors were former agents or former special operations personnel. He trusted them to know the boundaries. Then he chided himself for even giving Sofia McKay any credit. She was a troublemaker. Another headache he didn't need.

THE DRAMAMINE was working.

Scott Stiletto stood at a rail on the bow of the USS *Bataan*, feeling the up-and-down movement of the ship on the water, the blue ocean thrashing below him. Normally such motion and such a sight would make him vomit, but the pill he'd taken had settled his stomach.

He didn't know what to do with himself. He smoked a Hamlet cigar to pass the time, the hard wind blowing bits of ash in his face. He had orders to check in with the general every four hours. His next check-in was two hours away, and if the general had no further orders, that would be the end of their conversations until he returned to headquarters. As the wind blew, he knew that meant he would have a lot of time to himself. When that happened, his mind wandered.

He wasn't sure just why his daughter Felicia blamed him for the loss of her mother, Maddy. Her anger probably stemmed from his being gone a lot during the marriage on one overseas assignment or another, only retiring to a normal life just in time for his wife to pass. Maybe Felicia'd had hopes for a normal family life once her father settled down. Maybe she was upset at those dreams being shattered. Maybe she really didn't know her father, and here he was her only surviving parent, and she wasn't sure how to cope. Stiletto didn't think their relationship had been that bad, but one could never really tell what another was thinking or feeling until it was often too late to make a change.

Stiletto knew he could go in circles trying to figure out his daughter and he wouldn't be any closer to an answer than when she had cut off communication with him.

He tried, each year on her birthday and again at Christmas, to reach out, but she'd so far been unwilling to answer his calls.

His only distraction was to work, so he threw himself into The Job.

After Maddy died and Felicia went her own way, Stiletto had to find something to do. Taking a cushy job for a New York City private investigations firm suddenly lost its appeal, so he contacted a friend at CIA. An interview with a recruiter began the entry process. Six months later, after an exhausting series of interviews and background checks, Stiletto arrived at The Farm, the CIA's training center. It didn't take long for him to come to the attention of General Ike's unit.

The way he saw it, he was fighting for those who couldn't fight for themselves—the "forgotten victims" of the world who were forced into situations out of their control by powerful people who would kill them if they didn't comply. He was the powerful opposing force who was able to dish out the kind of punishment such animals deserved. At least it was a purpose. A reason to get out of bed every morning.

But in his less sober moments, he heard his daughter's voice asking why he just couldn't come home.

Maybe he really *was* the problem.

The ocean certainly held no answers. Stiletto puffed on his cigar, and watched waves crash into the hull, the hammering of the impacts unable to throw the ship off course. The irresistible force meeting the immovable object. Which one was he?

THE COMPUTER screen finally came to life. Stiletto sat up and clicked on the prompt to take the call, and the general's face filled the screen.

Stiletto didn't waste time with hellos.

"Anything new, General?"

"Indeed," General Ike said. "The tattoo picture turned out to be a godsend."

"Who was he?"

"Darius Porter. He has connections to militant radical groups, but was last known to be working for an arms dealer and mercenary colonel named Devlin Marcus."

"Never heard of him."

"He hides out in Italy. I'm forwarding his information,

and there's a chopper on the way to pick you up. If Porter is still working for Marcus, we need to bring him in. If not, Marcus needs to tell us who Porter was working for when he showed up in Iraq."

"Copy all, sir. And thanks."

CHAPTER EIGHT

DEVLIN MARCUS, according to the CIA's information, kept religiously to his habits, which included a nightly jaunt to the Casino Municipale di Campione d'Italia in Milan, Italy. The exterior resembled that of a fancy museum, with Lake Ceresio and mountains just beyond. Stiletto slid his rental car into an open space in the underground garage and followed a loud group of people to the elevators. When he emerged on the first floor, the wide-open space filled with slot machines greeted him with ringing, dinging, clicking, clacking, bells, whistles, and shouts of excitement. He might as well have been in Las Vegas. The noise was the same and slot machines are alike all over the world, and always irritating. The group he'd ridden up with added bursts of delight at the sight before them and converged on the machines like hungry ducks. They were quickly swallowed by the larger organism already in place.

Stiletto wandered across the floor. The casino filled a major part of Milan's very active nightlife, but he wasn't somebody who enjoyed such activity. His evenings, when not on assignment, were normally quiet, spent at home or visiting the neighborhood jazz club or playing poker with colleagues. He avoided large gatherings because mixing with a huge throng of rowdy individuals was not his idea of a good time.

Following a winding carpeted staircase to the second of the casino's nine floors, he glanced at a pair of young women in tight party outfits who wore their long black hair in almost identical waves. Their chattering kept them from noticing him. As Stiletto cleared the steps, he thought they could have been any average twenty-some-thing females in America, and decided the global spread of popular Western culture wasn't necessarily a good thing. Everybody looked and dressed like everybody else. Individual identity, if it had ever existed, was no match for the monster of conformity.

Presently Stiletto located the private poker room at the rear of the second floor, where he paid for a seat. He found a corner table with three players and two open chairs and selected a chair across from the man he knew to be Devlin Marcus.

Marcus wore the latest GQ International: plain black silk shirt, top button undone, black trousers, silver Rolex. His black hair seemed pasted to his head and dangled over the top of each ear. He brushed at either ear periodically.

The game was No Limit Texas Hold 'em. The current hand concluded with Marcus losing at least two small bets. The winner was a stocky Italian with dark eyes and hair.

The fourth man had lighter hair and covered his bulging middle with a black leather jacket. Stiletto handed the dealer paper notes in exchange for a stack of plaques and nodded hello to the other men.

"American?" Marcus said. He brushed at his right ear.

"Yes," Stiletto said.

"Good. I was getting lonely here." He grinned at the other two. "Us against them?"

The stocky man let out a low laugh, and the other man stared at Stiletto.

Stiletto said, "What happens when it's just us?"

Marcus shrugged. "I'm sure you'll be a good loser."

"Let's play some cards."

Stiletto bet the big blind on the first hand and folded when the clock came around to him again. He'd been dealt two low cards, and the other players bet too heavily for him to participate. The stocky man took the hand, and as the dealer cut the deck for the next round, Marcus brushed one of his ears. Stiletto noticed he did not do that during playing, probably so nobody would interpret it as a "tell."

Stiletto clicked his stack of blue plaques as the dealer dealt the next hand and looked at his cards as Marcus bet and the stocky man called. The light-haired man folded. Stiletto considered his cards some more.

Marcus said, "So?"

Stiletto called, and Marcus smiled. The dealer dropped the flop, three cards in the center of the table. Stiletto now had a pair of nines, one in hand and one on the table. Not bad, but nothing great, considering the next highest card on the table was a jack. If Marcus or the stocky Italian had another jack in hand, or maybe a pair in hand, he was already behind. The other card Stiletto held was a king; perhaps another nine or another king would show up in the river or the turn. Each man bet, and the dealer set down the next card. An ace. Marcus bet heavy and the stocky man raised. Stiletto folded. Marcus called. The dealer set down the last card. Another jack. Stiletto stifled a laugh. Marcus and the stocky man turned over their cards. The stocky man made a fist as Marcus scooped the chips his way. His two pair, jacks and aces, won the hand.

Marcus turned to Stiletto. "You gonna make me do all the work?"

Stiletto smiled and clicked his plaques. He played tight over the next several hands, winning a small pot with a high pair. He folded most hands, waiting for a big strike. He had a sense the strike had arrived when the dealer handed him a pair of aces. Stiletto bet light to start, letting the others call and raise, not wanting to risk too much money so early. If no other pairs or aces turned up on the table, it was all for naught.

The flop turned up a king and two low cards. Marcus bet heavy, and the two Italians called. Stiletto raised. His aces beat what was on the table. The others took the bait and matched him. The dealer turned up another ace, and Marcus hesitated a moment but bet anyway. The Italians called, as did Stiletto. The pot was sweet enough. When they turned over their cards, Stiletto's three of a kind beat the stocky man's two jacks, the next highest hand.

The dealer shuffled the cards. Stiletto and Marcus restacked their plaques.

Marcus said, "We make a fair team."

"It's you and me now."

"I didn't get your name."

"Jake Cooper." Stiletto rose and offered a hand across the table.

"Devlin Marcus. Call me Dev."

They shook. Marcus used a firm grip and did not break eye contact.

The dealer offered the deck to Stiletto, and Stiletto cut it. The dealer whipped a pair of cards to each player. Stiletto glanced down. A pair of sixes, non-suited. He glanced at Marcus, who pressed his lips together as he examined his own cards. Stiletto had not seen him press his lips together before. He bet some reds and blues, and Marcus called. The dealer dropped the flop. Two more sixes. Four of a kind for Stiletto, a good hand. The third card was a two, which meant nothing to Stiletto and wouldn't help Marcus, either. Stiletto checked. Marcus bet. Stiletto called and raised. Marcus pressed his lips together again.

"You have the other sixes?" Marcus asked.

"Maybe I want you to think so."

Marcus called.

The dealer set down the turn. A jack. Stiletto tapped

the table, checking. Marcus bet. At best he had three jacks, Stiletto decided, no match for his four sixes. Stiletto called. The dealer placed another jack on the table. Stiletto hesitated. If Marcus had the four jacks, the hand was over.

Stiletto said, "All in," and pushed his stacks toward the center of the table.

"Really?" said Marcus. "You gotta get to bed early or something?"

Stiletto folded his hands and watched his opponent.

"Okay, I'll bite." Marcus pushed all in.

"Turn 'em," Stiletto said, flipping over his two sixes. "Four of a kind."

Marcus's smile didn't fade as he tossed his cards toward the center. "Nice play." Marcus rose, shook Stiletto's hand again, and excused himself. Stiletto collected his plaques, tipped the dealer, and walked away from the table. The plastic plaques clicked in his pockets. He visited the cashier, where he exchanged the plaques for a little cash and the rest in a check. That meant a wait, but Stiletto didn't want his pockets bulging with paper money. He went up two floors, where he found a bar, selected a corner table, and ordered a Maker's and Coke.

STILETTO HAD half-finished a second drink when Devlin Marcus entered the bar, stopping when he noticed Stiletto. He smiled and approached the table. "May I join you?"

"Sure."

Marcus waved over a waitress and asked for a brandy and water.

Stiletto said, "I hope I didn't take your milk money."

"Chump change to me, don't worry," Marcus said. His drink arrived, and he raised his glass. "To *unsafe* bets."

Stiletto tapped the other man's glass. "What sort of business are you in?"

"Import and export. I ship stuff all over the world. Got a place on the lake about two miles from here."

Stiletto already knew that. "Miles?" he asked.

"You can take the Yank out of America and all that. What about you?"

"International consultant," Stiletto said. "Specializing in nefarious activities."

Marcus laughed. "You must be in demand."

"Between jobs right now."

"It's tough out there."

"I'll survive. Thought I might find some action here."

Marcus swallowed some of his drink. "Well, if I hear of any nefarious activity, I'll mention your name. It was fun playing cards with you. Routing the Eyeties never gets dull." He tossed back the rest of his drink. "You in town long?"

"Two or three more days."

Marcus stood. "Nice meeting you. You can pay for my drink." He grinned and departed.

STILETTO RODE down in the elevator and couldn't shake his disappointment. He had hoped to gain Marcus's confidence and get an invite into his operation. As a first meeting, it wouldn't have been bad, but Marcus made no attempt to learn where Stiletto was staying or how to reach him. Stiletto saw no defeat. He'd try again, this time the not-so-easy way.

The elevator doors rumbled open and Stiletto, alone, stepped into the garage and heard his own footsteps echo until more echoes joined his. Stiletto turned around. Three men approached. The middle one, who wore black-rimmed glasses, held an automatic pistol. He said, "Stop."

The gunman stepped too close. Stiletto launched a back-spin kick into the man's wrist. His wrist-bone cracked, and the gun went flying. The other two moved in. Stiletto stepped into the swing of the man on his left, intercepting the force of the man's forearm with his left shoulder. A two-finger strike to the man's throat sent him recoiling, choking, while the last man swung a blackjack. Stiletto bent back to avoid the swing, but not far enough, and the tip of the blackjack stung his nose. The third man swung again and Stiletto caught his wrist, twisting and forcing the man to bend with his arm. A follow-up blow to the solar plexus left the guy doubled over, sucking air.

Stiletto snatched up the fallen pistol. The man with the glasses had left the safety on. Stiletto clicked it off and covered the three groaning men, who began to cluster together in some sort of formation with Glasses up front.

"Nice try," Stiletto said. "Beat it."

"You don't—"

"I said go." Stiletto raised the gun to eye level for emphasis.

The trio limped and staggered away, Glasses glaring back. Stiletto held the gun steady. The men boarded an elevator, and the doors closed behind them.

Stiletto let out a breath. The tip of his nose throbbed like it was a big pulsing beacon. He touched it, but there wasn't any swelling. Maybe later. Dropping the gun in a trash can, he found his rental and drove away.

STILETTO DECIDED the trio made lousy hold-up men. Had Devlin Marcus sent them? Bright street lamps flashed light into the car, punctuating his thoughts. Had he hit a nerve with Marcus, or had the trio been watching the game the whole time?

Scott returned to his hotel and changed into dark jeans, a crew-neck shirt with long sleeves, and black steel-toed shoes with black socks. A brown leather shoulder holster with his gun on the left side under his arm and two spare ten-round extended magazines under his right completed the outfit. He covered the harness with a long jacket, the inside pockets of which contained other goodies he might require, such as a collapsible steel baton and a set of lock picks.

He stood in front of the mirror to make sure nothing showed and leaned close to look at the tip of his nose.

It was turning red. He stepped away and practiced two draws, bringing the Colt pistol to eye level and aiming at his nose.

Before leaving, he slipped his hotel key card into an envelope between two pieces of stationary and sealed the envelope. He asked the girl at the hotel desk to put the envelope in the office safe.

STILETTO SCALED a tree outside the wall around Marcus's large single-level home near the shore of Lake Ceresio. He heard the water lapping at the shore and appreciated the added element of clouds blocking the moonlight. A lone guard patrolled the yard, approaching Stiletto's position from the right. The guard moved close to the wall and had his hands free, so Stiletto figured he carried only a handgun.

Stiletto removed the baton from inside his coat. The guard passed, and Stiletto leaped from the tree and landed a few feet behind him. As the guard pivoted, Stiletto snapped the baton to full length and swung. The steel slammed into the side of the guard's head, and the man dropped in an unconscious heap. Stiletto dragged him behind a bush and checked for a radio, but found none. Stiletto scanned the yard as he pressed the baton back into its collapsed position and stowed it. The yard had no other places of cover, being only a wide expanse of trimmed grass. What looked like a gazebo sat in shadow beyond the house, which was dark.

The attached garage, also dark, seemed like the best point of entry. The cement driveway led from the garage door to a gate that faced the street. He left the bush at a run, increasing speed as he reached the middle of the yard. His shoes dug into the soft ground with each step and he slowed upon reaching the garage, stopping near a dark window and pressing his back to the wall. Presently he ducked below the window and moved to a side door.

A gentle breeze cooled the sweat on his neck as he examined the lock. A normal doorknob, nothing fancy, and no deadbolt. Did Marcus not go in for elaborate security? Then again, in an area so close to the general population, maybe he didn't want to be too obvious. Stiletto pulled out his lock picks, popped the lock, and put the picks away. He drew the Colt, snapped back the slide, and entered the garage.

Two cars, four-door sedans, faced the garage door; Stiletto worked his way around the front of each car. He was steps away from the inside door when the lights snapped on and the door opened. Stiletto squinted a little, raising his gun at the figure in the doorway. The outside door opened as well, and Stiletto froze at the familiar click-clack of a sub-machine gun. He lowered his gun as his eyes adjusted to the light. Devlin Marcus stood in the inside doorway holding a gun. The guard behind Stiletto held a nasty-looking but always reliable Uzi.

"This is a funny way to get a rematch, Mr. Cooper," Marcus said, "considering it was you who won."

CHAPTER NINE

KYLIE SARTO glanced at Robert Moray, who sat beside her at the small table. They were in Barcelona, having been smuggled into the country, along with the ZH4 canister, by NWRF contacts. Anybody who questioned their tourist status in Spain would find their papers in perfect order.

Moray hadn't said much during the journey from Iraq, both of them drained by the action and the loss of Porter. She let him have his silence. Both were hardened combat veterans of one side or another, this war or that, so Porter's loss was nothing new to them, but they had worked closely with the man, and he deserved more than just "what the hell."

They sat in Barcelona's Harlem Jazz Club, not far from their hotel, where Moray had wanted to go because jazz was his favorite type of music. Kylie wasn't so convinced. It was loud, brash, and repetitive. Give her Bach or Mozart any day.

The club was dark, narrow, and crowded. The audience facing the small stage sat around small tables, and the closeness of the walls made Kylie feel like she was trapped in an overcrowded coffin. Moray tapped his feet and watched the band with great excitement, sipping from a glass of bourbon on the rocks.

The glass of wine in front of her remained mostly untouched. It was the house wine, and it was gross.

The mission had at least been successful so far, and they were in Barcelona to meet a contact who would give them their next instructions. They had been a couple for at least six months, having met at an NWRF training camp. They had been inseparable ever since. She found Moray magnetically attractive and hoped he thought the same of her. She wasn't sure where they were going, but she looked forward to getting there. She knew he had insisted on her being part of this mission, and that thrilled her. Maybe they had a nice future ahead.

Presently they left the club arm-in-arm and strolled along the still-busy sidewalk despite the late (or early) hour. Kylie didn't bother checking her watch. Streetlights blazed. The night was warm. They wore light jackets, but really didn't need them. Late-night bar-hoppers moved up and down the sidewalk, although traffic was light.

"When did you start listening to jazz?" she said.

"My uncle had a record collection," Moray said. "This big cabinet full of vinyl. It was wonderful, and when I'd visit, he'd have me select what he played. I was too young to really know, so I just pointed at stuff. He never seemed to mind."

"Ever play in a band yourself?"

Basic questions, Kylie thought, but then in their short time together, they'd never had a conversation like this.

"Garage band in high school," Moray said. "I played bass. Haven't touched an instrument since then."

He fell silent as they walked some more. Kylie wasn't entirely sure what his background was, but he was an American who had served in the US military, and now seemed more than eager to turn against the country of his birth. She, meanwhile, had no country that she considered her home. Italy, where she was born, had no more meaning for her than any other name on a map. She hoped, through the efforts of the NWRF, to rewrite that map entirely.

She'd grown up with her father, a lawyer and a Marxist, enthralling her from a young age with stories of the Communist Revolution. Her writings for left-wing publications at Paris Sorbonne brought her to the attention of one of the many factions on campus recruiting students, which later led to the more militant underground groups peppered throughout Europe, and ultimately to the New World Revolutionary Front.

"I can't believe we left that canister in the hotel," she exclaimed.

"It's fine," he assured her.

She squeezed his arm. "I'd be having a panic attack."

Moray smiled. "It's all under control."

They returned to the Serras and rode the elevator up to their room. The suite had a sunken living area, adjoining bedroom, and a floor-to-ceiling wrap-around window looking out on the city. The city lights twinkled in the night. Moray flipped on some lights and checked a closet, where the ZH4 canister sat undisturbed. Kylie removed her jacket and draped it on the back of a chair.

"So, what happens tomorrow?" she said. "You really haven't said much since we arrived."

Moray, at the window with hands in his pockets, turned. "I know."

"Iraq was pretty bad."

"Yes, it was."

"Are you worried about the Americans?"

Moray finally took off his jacket and flung it onto the nearby couch. "Want some coffee?"

"Sure."

Standing in the narrow hall near the door as the coffee brewed, they watched the percolator like a television. Kylie waited for Moray to continue. The wall of confidence he had shown prior to Iraq was still there on the surface, but along with that he now seemed overly cautious, as if he were afraid to state what he had in mind for their next move.

"Our contact," he finally said, "will meet us tomorrow, and then we're off to the US."

"You're sure?"

"That's all I'm sure of."

"Does that bother you?"

"A little. I like to know everything in advance."

"Like what we're doing with the nerve gas?"

"Exactly. We didn't grab it to decorate a mantle."

"Are you having doubts?"

"No," Moray said. "I just like to know things."

"I'd like to know something."

"What?"

"Why are you doing this? We're obviously going to use the nerve gas somewhere in the US, and you're from there. I'd think Zolac would have picked somebody else just in case you got cold feet."

"I volunteered."

"Why?"

"I gave my life to the US military," Moray said, "I was a good soldier, and they betrayed me."

"How?"

"Never mind how."

Moray poured two cups of coffee. She took hers black, same as he did. They sat on the couch..

"That wasn't my first time in Iraq," he said. "The last time ended almost the same way, except more men died. I was supposed to be one of them."

"But you lived."

He nodded, swallowing some French roast. He said nothing more. He seemed to want silence, so she let him have exactly that. Her ears still rang from the live music at the club, and the silence was actually kind of nice.

When she finished the last of her coffee, she stood. "I'm taking a shower before bed."

He nodded.

In the bathroom, she turned on the water and stripped off her clothes, leaving them in a pile on the tiled floor. Kylie ran her fingers through her short red hair, which still felt dirty after playing in the desert.

She stood under the water for a few minutes, letting it cascade down her body, then the curtain moved. Startled, she turned to see Moray, naked, stepping into the shower. The hair on his broad chest had touches of gray and a few scars stood out, but none of that mattered as a rush of desire ran through her body.

"You might use all the hot water," he said, reaching for her.

MARCUS LED Stiletto into a well-decorated den with white walls and tan carpet. Books filled the shelves, and paintings adorned the walls. At a small bar, Marcus poured Sailor Jerry's into a glass, then added Coca-Cola and handed the drink to Stiletto.

"You can't say I doped it," Marcus said, "since you saw me make it."

Stiletto took the glass and sat in a leather chair, black, before Marcus's desk. There was a matching chair behind the desk, and Marcus sat there after mixing a brandy and soda. Stiletto's gun, minus the magazine, was on the blotter. Stiletto expressed no surprise that he wasn't tied up or that Marcus had told the guard to leave. He took a drink instead.

Marcus picked up the Colt. "Nice gun. I prefer Smith & Wesson myself. I've been expecting you, Mr. Cooper, or whatever your name is. Knew who you were the moment you sat at the table tonight. You came to either capture or kill me."

Stiletto responded by taking another drink.

"You may be disappointed in my security, but I turned most of it off tonight in anticipation of your arrival. We do need to have an important talk."

"Why?"

"Because I know all about the ZH4 nerve gas and what happened in Iraq."

Stiletto waited.

"I sent those three men you tangled with in the casino's garage," Marcus said. "I should have said something, but considering the situation, you might not have believed me." Marcus brushed his left ear.

"There was a man in Iraq who had a tattoo on his neck. Darius Porter was his name. He was one of your people."

"You speak in the past tense."

"Because he's dead."

Marcus let out a sigh and glanced solemnly into his drink. "I told him that would happen."

"So you sent him?"

Marcus looked up sharply. "No. He quit my organization several months ago. Worse, he tried to take more people with him. I smuggle stuff and I hire out mercenaries, and we get a lot of interesting people. Sometimes they're worth keeping, sometimes they aren't."

"Was Porter worth keeping?"

"He had experience, sure, but he had delusions."

"Mental problems?"

"Not unless you think his idea of creating a global fascist state is a mental problem."

"Was that what he wanted?"

Marcus nodded. "He was less interested in fighting for money, and more interested in fighting for a cause. I blame his girlfriend."

"Who's she?"

"I never got her right name, but she started filling his head about 'the cause' and world revolution, etcetera—the usual garbage our grandfathers fought about that should be on the ash heap of history by now."

"And he found a group that supported that cause?"

Another nod. "She led him to it. I tried to stop him."

"You can't control what people do," Stiletto replied.

"Tell Porter," Marcus suggested.

Stiletto sipped his drink. "What do you know about the group he joined?"

"They call themselves the New World Revolutionary Front."

Stiletto lowered his glass with a frown. The name meant nothing to him.

"I did some research," Marcus said, "on the idea that maybe the information would be of use to somebody, and here you are."

"We appreciate anything you can provide."

"Appreciation doesn't pay my bills," Marcus said.

"You *are* a mercenary."

They laughed.

"You'll be compensated for your effort," Stiletto said. "Probably our standard fee, as long as the information is accurate and helps us find this group. They're running around with a canister of deadly nerve gas. I need to find them."

"Of course."

"So what do you know?"

"They're recruiting from everywhere," Marcus said. "Mercs like Porter. From the radical underground groups, the militant ones who talk a lot about overthrowing governments but never seem to have the cash. They've been active in Africa, looking for troops from the criminal syndicates. The Balkans, same thing. Elsewhere, I'm sure."

"And this group is well-funded?"

"Oh, indeed. I'm not sure where the money comes from, however."

"What are you sure of?"

"One of their commanders is named Heinrich Zolac. Mean anything to you?"

Stiletto shook his head.

"You might want to look him up," Marcus said.

"Sounds like you know more than you're telling."

"Sure, but why spoil all your fun?"

Stiletto raised his glass. "A man after my own heart."

He drank some more to cover his true reaction. Marcus was playing games, and Stiletto didn't like that.

He finished his drink and rose from the chair. Marcus stood as well and handed back the Colt. Stiletto holstered the pistol and the two men shook hands, never breaking eye contact. For all Scott knew, Marcus was as bad as the man Zolac he mentioned, but that was the spy business. Sometimes you needed a bad guy to catch a bad guy.

CHAPTER TEN

MORAY AND Kylie sat at a corner table in the back of the hotel restaurant waiting for their contact. Moray had no idea who to expect, only that they were to exchange a passcode.

When Moray looked across the restaurant at the tall figure of Heinrich Zolac, he knew no passcode would be required.

But rules were rules.

Moray pointed him out to Kylie as Zolac waved off a hostess and approached the table. He carried nothing and wore a sharply pressed suit and a purple tie.

"I hear it's snowing in Frankfurt," Zolac said.

"It only snows in July," Moray replied.

Zolac cracked a smile and pulled an extra chair from a neighboring empty table without prompting. He sat. Moray gestured to the appetizer sample plate in the center of the table and waved a waitress over. Zolac asked for ice water with lemon.

Moray sipped a beer. "I wasn't expecting you."

"It was more efficient for me to be here," Zolac said,

glancing at them both, "because we can keep the details within a closed loop. And another reason that I'll provide in a moment."

Moray nodded.

"Our leader is pleased with your work," Zolac said, "but he is disappointed that you are one short."

"We'll manage."

"You'll need a third man for when the operation reaches its climax," Zolac said. "I've volunteered. You're to do the setup and preparation, and I'll arrive prior to the execution."

"Okay."

Kylie's eyes moved quickly from Zolac to Moray, but he couldn't read her thoughts. Did she disapprove?

Zolac didn't look at her as he handed Moray an envelope from the inside of his jacket. While Moray opened the envelope, Zolac helped himself to a baked potato skin with a dollop of sour cream and bacon bits and melted cheese. The waitress returned with his water.

Moray scanned the two plane tickets and held up a USB thumb drive.

"We're not talking in the open," Zolac said. "I put a recording with photographs on the thumb drive."

"California?" Moray said, reading the tickets.

"Ever been there?"

"No."

Zolac swallowed another potato skin and drank some

water. "No need to contact me after you watch the recording. It's all there."

Moray nodded.

"Good luck."

Zolac rose and departed without a handshake.

Moray returned the items to the envelope and shoved it into the left pocket of his jeans. "Something wrong?"

"I don't like him," she said.

"He's number two in the outfit," Moray said. "You don't have to like him, but you have to listen to him."

"You might be listening, lover, but you aren't thinking. Why do we need help?"

Moray shrugged. "Getaway? Other details?"

"Once this operation starts," she said, "we'll be loose ends. He'll be there to clean up. Porter's job was to kill us."

Moray finished his beer in two swallows. "You're paranoid. Come on, let's go back to the room and watch this video."

Moray stood, but Kylie remained seated. She rotated her unfinished glass of red wine by the stem.

"Kylie. Now."

With a sigh, she followed him out. He entered the elevator first and pressed the button for their floor, and the elevator doors rumbled shut. He watched the floor indicator above the door. The numbers lit for a moment as the car ascended the levels.

Loose ends. The words bounced back and forth in his head.

He didn't look at Kylie, but he felt her looking at him. Loose ends.

He was blindly following orders again, not listening to his gut or the smart words of someone else. Last time his team had ended up dead because he didn't listen.

But what to do about it?

The elevator stopped, and the doors opened on their floor.

"You're right," he told Kylie. He exited first.

"WHAT DO we do?" she said. Kylie sat on the edge of the bed.

Moray paced.

"Do we quit and tell the Americans?" she said.

"No. No way. We're finishing the mission, but if Zolac thinks killing us will close the loop, the only thing we can do is kill him first. We can blame it on the US."

"Not until we're sure."

Moray glared at her. "You just said—"

She stopped him with a raised hand. "I'm not killing one of our people in cold blood. We'll know to be ready, and if it happens, we'll take action."

"All right."

She left the bed, and they held onto each other tightly for a moment. Moray pushed her away and went to the table where the laptop sat. He powered on the machine and sat. Kylie moved behind him to massage his shoulders.

Moray plugged in the thumb drive and opened the

video file contained on the stick.

Green grass, trees. The camera pulled back to show a park occupying a full square block with a gray stone building at one end.

Zolac's voice came over the speakers.

"Berkeley, California. The heart of the radical movement in the US, but they've never managed more than a noisy protest and a riot or two. They will be our pawns, sacrificed for the greater good.

"You are to find a suitable spot for the ZH4 and set it for release no later than two p.m. a week from today at this park. It's Civic Center Park near the city court buildings and police headquarters. We have organizers in the city preparing what they think is another protest against the outrageousness coming from Washington DC. Already, elements of the right wing, who have sent counter-protestors to several rallies around the nation, are planning to show up and declare their opposition. As with those other rallies, we expect a clash. Plenty of violence.

"Once the gas is released, we have people in the media ready to show proof that the right-wing agitators are responsible. The death toll will be huge. It is our goal that public opinion will turn against the conservative party in power and allow us to insert our own people. They are already standing by.

"After that, phase two begins, but at this time, that is none of your concern."

The video ended.

Moray sat still while Kylie kneaded his shoulders, his senses tingling from the touch of her slender fingers.

"I'm thinking car bomb," he said.

Kylie leaned close. He felt her hot breath on his neck.

"I'm thinking something else," she said. "Meet me in the shower in two minutes."

She moved quickly away, and Moray closed the laptop.

STILETTO RETURNED to his hotel in Milan after his meeting with Devlin Marcus, logged onto the CIA's secure information servers via his laptop, and spent time compiling data based on what the mercenary colonel had told him. The next morning, as he finished breakfast in his room, he addressed the general over Skype.

"Looks like we're facing a group calling itself the New World Revolutionary Front. Mean anything to you, sir?"

"Never heard of them."

Stiletto explained his meeting with Marcus, then went on, "They're minor players that have popped up now and then, but I think the reason they've stayed off our radar is that they've mostly robbed banks in Europe, with varying degrees of success. A few have been arrested for those robberies but have kept quiet about the goings-on.

"The reported leader is a man named Heinrich Zolac, but nothing I've found connects him to any violent groups. Marcus says somebody else provides the money, and I can't find anything on that, either."

"What did you learn about Zolac?"

"Billionaire. Developed silly games for mobile devices. Tech crowd loves him."

Stiletto sipped from a cup of tea.

"He's German," Scott continued, "and wrote for some radical newspapers and websites before he started with computers. He has a mansion in Austria just outside Vienna. Well-guarded. But he's not there now. He's checked into a resort in Monte Carlo, having just arrived from Barcelona."

"All we have to go on is what Marcus said? Nothing suspicious? Nothing that connects Zolac to the militant underground?"

"Nothing, sir. If I try to find him in Monte Carlo, it's a fishing expedition, and we have no idea how far along the enemy's clock is regarding the use of the ZH4."

Fleming said nothing for a moment. He blinked a few times, and his gaze drifted off-screen. Something wasn't right, Stiletto thought. The boss was more preoccupied than usual. Then the general said: "Who's in charge of the resort?"

Stiletto consulted a sheet of notes. "The resort is operated by a Russian woman named Elisa Yanovna. Ex-FSB. A corporation owns the place, but nothing connects it to Zolac."

"You weren't kidding about fishing. How concrete do you think Marcus' information is?"

"He believed it," Stiletto said. "He seemed to have a vested interest in knowing who was taking one of his men, and why that same individual was trying to recruit more to follow him."

Fleming nodded. "All right. We don't have anything else. You go to Monte Carlo. Meanwhile, I'll also put the Austrian place under surveillance."

"Copy that, sir, I'll leave this afternoon."

"Okay."

"You're not yourself, boss. What's going on back home?"

"Is it obvious?"

"We've worked together for too long, General."

"We have a reporter sniffing around, a woman named Sofia McKay. She's talking around town about our contractors in Saudi Arabia torturing terror suspects."

"One of those, huh?"

Fleming explained his research into the woman's past activities. "I don't mind telling you," he added, "that I'm suspicious of her appearance at this time."

"Why?"

"First we have the theft of the ZH4, and now she shows up. It's almost as if somebody knows we might take an interest and wants to throw a wrench into the works."

"If you'd rather I come back home to help—"

"Stay on task. We're okay here. Legal is preparing a response, but we're ready for a hearing if what she publishes brings us to that. We don't have anything to hide."

"The other side always says we do, sir. And for some reason, they're believed more often than we are."

"We lie for a living, Scott. It's not hard to understand. Get back with me when you have something."

"Will do."

Stiletto ended the call.

SCOTT STEERED the rented Jaguar F-Type Coupe along the twisting two-lane road leading to Monte Carlo's Cairo Resort, a large casino hotel with Egyptian-style architecture. Off to the left, ocean waves slammed the coastal beach, the bright sun creating a shimmer on the water.

The Jag's engine purred as Scott goosed the throttle around the last turn, and the towering Cairo Resort came into view, one tall building with dozens of smaller surrounding structures on the slope of a mountain, all overlooking the ocean.

Stiletto slowed as he turned into the parking lot and pulled in behind a line of cars in the valet lane. Presently a uniformed young man took the car. Stiletto refused help with his two suitcases and checked in.

The lobby tile and the marble walls had tiny diamonds embedded in them that sparkled in the bright light from tall windows facing the sea. The glitz was everywhere, in the tiniest detail. The elevator took Stiletto to his floor. He had booked one of the rooms at the front of the hotel, the expensive high-roller side, because of the ocean view, but Stiletto immediately wanted his money back when the blinding sun coming through the window overwhelmed both the room and the view. He kept the drapes closed.

Stiletto unpacked, filling the dresser drawers and closet with clothes and leaving out airline tickets and a small black book containing the coded names and phone numbers of known operators in the underground mercenary community. Stiletto's "Jake Cooper" cover identity would check out if anybody on that list was asked about him. Eventually, if his fishing turned up any bites, the opposition would search his room, and he wanted those items found.

The only personal item he brought was his sketchbook. He set that on the writing table.

From the X-ray proof bottom of his larger suitcase, he took out a box of Federal Hydra-Shok JHP ammo, three magazines, and his custom-built Colt Combat Government pistol.

He had one other gadget—a belt with a slit on the inside holding a razor blade that had come in handy more than once when he needed to cut through ropes.

No rich mercenary would walk around without his hardware.

STILETTO TOOK some time to wander around the resort.

Tennis courts, swimming pools, shops, spas. Everything a modern resort required.

He frowned when a pattern developed among the guests. The average tourist was easy to spot, but there were others amongst the clientele who didn't belong. These men and women were younger, fitter, and demonstrated a sense of awareness of their surroundings that the Europeans and fat Americans did not. Obviously, they could be members of the new jet set, gallivanting around the world on grandpa's money, but Stiletto dismissed the idea that they were all part of that. The ones who caught his attention looked like military personnel, but no GI Scott had served with could ever have afforded the Cairo Resort.

Stiletto treated himself to a deep-tissue massage at the spa. The petite blonde masseuse noted his bumps and bruises and tried to strike up a conversation about them, but Stiletto didn't give her much to work with. He said he'd been roughed up surfing, and eventually, she stopped trying to engage him. He let his mind wander as she worked the knots out of his back and shoulders. When he left, he felt ten times better—relaxed, loosened up, and ready for the night.

After the massage, he found the resort's smoking lounge and picked up a box of Montecristo cigars—the Cuban variety this time—and lit up with gusto as he eased into a plush leather chair. At home, he could only afford the Dominican Montecristos, which he actually preferred, but nobody who had access to the Cubans would pass them up.

He only half-listened to the conversation from the three other occupants until somebody started talking cars, then he jumped in and ended up telling tales of his restoration efforts. They all agreed that if it weren't for their cars, they'd be rich.

Later that night at the hotel restaurant, he ordered a steak and potato dinner. He'd asked for a corner table and sat with his back to the oak-paneled wall. The steak was rare, no sauce, and the potato dripped butter and was covered with bacon bits. Not the healthiest, but he didn't care.

He sat forward in his chair. He wore the .45 in an inside-the-waistband holster, and the gun dug into his back and rear if he sat all the way back. Ah, the glamour of undercover work. Nobody ever saw that on tv.

He looked around at the other patrons—couples, solos, and families. The families were the hardest ones to look at. He never could have afforded to take Maddy and Felicia to a place like this, but he wished he'd had the chance. He wished a lot of things when they strayed into his thoughts.

Stiletto finished dinner and entered the casino. He went straight for a blackjack table, ordered a Maker's Mark with a splash of water from a passing waitress, and smiled at the dealer. She was a young woman with long curly hair and hoop earrings. Her uniform fit loosely.

She told Scott he could join on the next hand. A lone woman sat at the table, and she stood on her current hand. She turned her cards over and showed nineteen. The dealer produced seventeen. The woman collected her three hundred-euro plaques as well as the house's and walked away.

The dealer did not speak as she opened and shuffled a new deck. Stiletto cut and she shuffled again. Stiletto placed two hundred-euro plaques on the table, and she matched him. She dealt two cards and took two for herself.

Scott peeked at his hand. Five of diamonds; six of spades. Eleven in total.

"Hit," he said.

The dealer dealt another card. Three of hearts. Fourteen now. Worth a chance. He asked for another card.

Jack of hearts.

"I bust," he told the dealer.

He showed his cards. Twenty-four.

The dealer flipped. "Dealer has eighteen." She pulled the four plaques to her side. "Again?"

"One more time." He bet another two hundred and received his cards after another shuffle-cut-shuffle.

He had a four of hearts and four of diamonds. "Hit."

The dealer slapped down another card. Ten of spades. "Stay."

The dealer examined her cards, hit once, then again. "Stay," she said.

Stiletto flipped over his cards. "Eighteen."

"Seventeen," she said, and passed him the plaques.

"Go again," he told her.

The dealer shuffled, and Scott cut. They placed bets,

and the dealer handed out cards. Scott had a nine and a jack.

"Stay."

The dealer hit once and stood. So did Stiletto. They turned over. Each had nineteen, a push. Stiletto let the bet ride, and they played another hand.

OVER THE next hour, the stack of plaques on Stiletto's left grew higher.

Soon it became two stacks of 100-euro plaques. Stiletto lost a little but gained it back with some effort.

Spectators formed around the table, but Stiletto ignored them. The concentration made him sweat, and he wiped his forehead with a handkerchief often.

The winning did not go unnoticed, and eventually, the pit boss wandered over and pushed through the crowd. He watched for a few hands, Stiletto winning two and losing one, then he withdrew. Scott pretended not to see the man and kept playing.

CHAPTER ELEVEN

THE PIT boss went to the bar.

He told the bartender he needed the direct line, and the bartender brought up a phone from under the counter. The pit boss pressed two buttons and waited.

"I have a player at table 12, an American. He's beating the house. Shall I close the table?"

The pit boss listened a moment and hung up. The bartender put the phone back under the counter.

The pit boss walked back to the table where the spectators let out a low cheer as the player won another hand. The pit boss pushed through the crowd and drew a hand across his throat to stop the dealer from shuffling. The woman put down the cards.

Stiletto turned to the pit boss. "What's the problem?"

"I'm closing the table."

"But I'm not tired of winning yet."

"The table is closed, please move along."

The spectators faded. Scott rose. He was the same height as the pit boss.

"You think I was cheating?"

"Please move along before we escort you out."

"I'm a paying guest at this resort." Stiletto stepped closer.

"Sir—"

Stiletto made a grab for the holstered gun under the pit boss's coat. The man reacted too slowly, his hands barely reaching Stiletto's wrist before Scott jammed the gun into the man's belly.

"Let's go see your boss."

The pit boss swallowed. "What are you doing?"

"Getting an escort to the top floor. Now start walking."

THE PIT boss exited an elevator.

Stiletto, still holding the gun, walked behind him. They stepped into a well-appointed office. It was very warm. A woman sat behind a desk. The window behind her looked out on the brightly-lighted city.

"What's going on?"

The woman rose. She had long dark hair that fell in waves; short black skirt and a purple silk top that fit tightly.

"Elisa Yanovna, I presume," Scott said.

"Who are you?"

Stiletto stepped around the pit boss and handed back the gun.

"My apologies, but I didn't think I could just walk up here."

Elisa Yanovna dismissed the pit boss, who got back into the elevator.

A door to Stiletto's left opened and a burly bald man entered. He carried no weapon, but his size and the strength he projected told Stiletto he'd be a tough opponent. The man stood by the door with hands clasped in front of him.

Stiletto turned back to the woman. "My name is Jake Cooper. I'm a merc looking for a job."

"I don't know what a merc is."

Stiletto glanced at the other man, whose still expression communicated his ignorance of a "merc" too.

The woman nodded at the other man, who approached Stiletto and patted him down. He did not touch Stiletto's back. As the man stepped away, Stiletto said, "Behind my back." The man checked there and took the Colt. He resumed his original position.

The woman folded her arms and put her weight on one leg.

"It's illegal to carry a gun here," she said. "You could go to jail."

"I have skills I know you'll appreciate."

"I have enough dealers, but I could use somebody on the janitorial staff."

The other man laughed. Stiletto thought it was funny too.

"Let's stop the joking," Scott said. "We both know the score, Ms. Yanovna. If there really are no openings, I'll move on, no hard feelings."

"I'll have to make a few calls, Mr. Cooper. Before we talk further."

"Great. Finally."

Yanovna said, "Say hello to my number two, Viktor Plotkin."

Stiletto nodded at the other man but made no move to shake hands. Yanovna made a gesture and Plotkin handed back Stiletto's gun.

"What about the money I won?"

"It will be delivered to your room, don't worry. You won't lose a penny."

Stiletto let silence fill the room and watched the pair stare at him a moment.

"I guess I'll see myself out," Stiletto said. He stepped back into the elevator and waved as the doors slid shut.

ELISA YANOVNA folded her arms.

Plotkin left his spot and poured a drink at the small bar in the corner. He handed the vodka to the woman and poured another.

Yanovna took a drink, but her eyes never left the elevator.

Plotkin said, "It's awfully strange, isn't it? He shows up just days after the operation starts."

Elisa said nothing.

"Do you recognize his name?"

"Doesn't sound familiar, but that doesn't mean anything. Check him out. I don't want to mention this to Zolac until we actually know something."

"He's trouble. This is not a good idea."

"Do what I tell you," she said. "We need to be careful,

not paranoid."

Plotkin glared, finished his drink, and put the glass down on the bar. He returned to his office.

Elisa Yanovna sat down again and considered several possible scenarios. If this man was on the level, she probably could use him if Zolac didn't need him elsewhere. If he was an American agent attempting to infiltrate, it meant the NWRF wasn't as bulletproof as Zolac liked to believe, and that put them all at risk.

But in the end, she only worked for Zolac. He'd listen to her opinion and do whatever he wanted. She at least had to know more. That was the first step. With Plotkin on that detail, answers were not far away.

THEY WOULD be watching him from here forward.

Scott skipped further casino play for a seat at a bar instead. He ordered a Maker's on the rocks. He did not select a corner table despite his better judgment, relying on the bar's mirror to help him cover his back.

A trio entered the bar, talking and laughing. Stiletto saw them in the mirror. All three were males, thin and muscular with short haircuts. Too tanned for average tourists. More soldier-types? What had attracted so many of them to the Cairo Resort?

Stiletto finished his drink and ordered another. He checked his watch. Plotkin would need a two-hour window to cover Scott's room. Stiletto figured he wouldn't have trouble filling the time.

SUNNY SKIES greeted Robert Moray and Kylie Sarto as they stepped off the Delta 737 at Oakland International Airport.

They did not travel under their real names and had employed mild disguises.

Kylie wore a wig-and-scarf combo, a brunette this time, the pink scarf wrapped loosely over the neck of her leather jacket.

Moray couldn't remove any of his bulk or height, but he could alter his face a little, with a goatee and mustache, each touched with a little gray, with the bottom of his right shoe filed off to give him a slight limp. The little things counted.

They left the airport property in a rental and followed Interstate 880 north. Zolac had secured a safe house for them to operate from. Kylie plugged the address into the car's in-dash GPS, and a voice with a British accent directed them along the route.

Kylie glanced at Moray, who kept his eyes focused ahead, scanning traffic. He wouldn't talk during the drive because he was driving. He needed total concentration. It made her laugh.

She turned up the heater as Moray sped along just under the highway limit. The dashboard temperature gauge said it was sixty-eight degrees outside.

"We should go to San Francisco and see the sights," she said.

Moray only grunted.

Presently Moray made the connection to Eastbound Interstate 80, turned off the freeway at the University Avenue exit and they followed a route to the suburbs, where the narrow streets dipped on either side to help keep standing water from accumulating on the pavement. Yards were full of lush green lawns, and the multiple colors of a wide variety of flowers kept Kylie's attention as they moved.

Moray finally slowed and turned into a driveway cluttered with leaves, a raised crack a few feet from the sidewalk. Moray let the front wheels go over the crack and stopped the car. He and Kylie regarded the small house before them curiously.

"This is better than a hotel?" Moray said.

The house had puke-green paint, a large porch, and a brick chimney. Messy yard. The grass was overgrown, and half-dead bushes and trees covered most of the porch.

"I'm sure it's nice inside," Kylie said. They left the car and carried their bags into the house. "See?" she said. "Much better."

The interior was the exact opposite: wood floors, white walls, and every room furnished with antique-looking items that Kylie said provided a certain charm to the place. Moray went to the kitchen and tested the faucet in the sink. Cold water ran strong. He investigated the hallway bathroom as well, turning on the shower a moment. He came out of the hall wiping a wet hand on his pants.

"It will do," he said. "At least we're not paying for it."

They found the master bedroom at the very end of the hall and loaded the dresser with their clothes.

"We should hit the store for supplies," Moray said.

"I'll make a list."

She investigated cupboard and refrigerator space in the kitchen, finding more than enough room. Usual counter, kitchen table, and a separate breakfast nook near a window looking out on a backyard as equally overgrown as the front. More wood and white, no attention to other colors or decorative arrangements.

"A man owns this," Kylie said to herself.

A blast of air rumbled through the vents. "Heater works," Moray announced.

It was as good a safe house as they could want, Kylie decided. The yard out front partially concealed the living room windows, offering plenty of cover for their activities. And because it was ugly in front, nobody would pay much attention to what happened within. A nosy neighbor might bring over a pie to welcome them to the block, but they could deal with that.

Kylie removed her wig and scarf, running fingers through her red hair to bring it back to life. She made a grocery list and started for the front door. Stepping onto the porch, something skittered off to her left. She saw the back end of a cat slither under the porch rail to hide in the bushes. The cat peered back at her through the leaves.

"Hi," she said. She squatted down. The cat, tense, stared at her. "Do you live here too?" The cat's eyes stayed fixed on her. The animal looked very bony and thin, with no body mass. She looked over the warped wood of the porch, the peeled paint, cracks. She could put out a bowl of food. The cat slid under the porch, its long tail the last thing to vanish beneath the wood. Kylie stood and went to the car. Driving away, she wondered if she should tell Moray about the cat. She wasn't sure he even liked cats.

PLOTKIN SLIPPED a keycard into Stiletto's lock.

He stepped inside and checked the closet first, then the bathroom. Nobody hiding. It seemed silly to start off that way, but Plotkin hadn't survived for so long in the game of international espionage by being stupid. Silly, yes.

He searched the dresser but found only clothes and a plane ticket for a return trip to Athens on the nightstand. A black book lay askew next to the phone, and he flipped through the pages. The names and numbers were coded. He put the book in a pocket.

The Russian looked around some more, but it was all perfectly boring. Almost too boring.

CHAPTER TWELVE

VIKTOR PLOTKIN tossed the black book on Elisa Yanovna's desk. It landed with a slap.

"He knows it's missing by now," Plotkin said.

"Does he check out?"

Plotkin had worked late into the previous night and part of the morning on his research, calling the familiar names in the book and asking about one Jake Cooper. "Yes. He's clean as far as I can tell."

"I'll give it back tonight."

"What happens tonight?" Plotkin said.

"Zolac wants to meet him and play poker."

"That is a mistake."

"You said he checks out."

"What if I'm wrong? Bring him here to tell him about meeting Zolac. Let him see your safe. If he is here to look for information, he'll look there. If we catch him—"

Elisa Yanovna folded her arms and leaned back in her chair. She kept her eyes locked on Plotkin's face.

"We have to be sure, Elisa."

She looked through the black book. She recognized

a few names, but not all of them. If Cooper knew those operatives, he had to be all right.

"Okay." She put the book back on her desk. "We'll do one last check. If he goes for the safe, we'll know he's a spy."

STILETTO SAT up in bed, drawing in his sketchbook. Part of a cliff took shape, then the ocean below, and a woman atop the cliff looking over the edge. He figured something should be in the water for her to look at, so he added a dragon, the scratching of his pencil on the paper filling the quiet room as if it were a private symphony just for him.

Somebody knocked, breaking the spell. Stiletto put the sketch aside and answered. Plotkin stood in the hallway. "Miss Yanovna wants to see you."

"Sure," Stiletto said. He was already dressed and packing the .45 behind his back. It amused him a great deal that his black book had been taken. Sometimes, the enemy was as predictable as the sunrise. He wondered how many calls they had made. If his cover didn't hold up to that cursory check, he'd be walking to his death.

He locked the room and followed Plotkin down the hall.

"I'M SORRY we stole your book," Elisa said. "Here it is."

Stiletto stowed the black book inside his jacket. "I checked out?"

She only smiled.

Stiletto sat in front of her desk while Plotkin paced the carpet behind him.

"You're a good blackjack player," she said. "Can you handle poker?"

Stiletto grinned. "Fairly well."

"Good. Mr. Zolac wants to meet you, and he likes to play."

Elisa grabbed a stack of folders from her desk and went over to a painting on the wall, which she opened like a door, to reveal a safe. He admired her figure as she spun the dial. He also watched the combination and tried not to laugh. She put the folders in the safe with other items, closed the safe, and put the painting back in place.

Stiletto glanced at Plotkin, who was watching him. Stiletto smiled and did not break eye-contact. When Elisa returned to her desk, Stiletto put his attention back on her.

"How much money do I need for tonight?" Scott said.

"Oh, five thousand US should do it."

"No problem."

"Don't let Mr. Zolac win," she said. "He expects everybody to play their best."

"I won't let him down," Stiletto said.

ANOTHER MAKER'S with a splash of water.

Only regular tourists in the bar this time, no off-duty NWRF troops, and this time Stiletto occupied a back-corner table. He laughed as the image of Elisa and her safe replayed in his mind. Did they think he was a first-year rookie? Who but a nimrod would fall for such an obvious carrot?

It meant they weren't positive that he was genuine. Or maybe they *were* sure, but this was one last test. He remembered that Plotkin had watched him during Elisa's display. She was convinced; *he* wasn't. Regardless, Stiletto had no plans to take the bait.

He left the bar to get some lunch and bought a pack of playing cards from the gift shop. He spent the rest of the day reviewing poker hands and mentally preparing to meet the man he figured was the top dog in the New World Revolutionary Front.

ELISA KNOCKED on Stiletto's door.

She wore her hair down, with black slacks and a sparkly black-and-white top with a V-neck. There was a small scar above her right breast. She looked quite desirable, and Stiletto cleared his throat. Was he ready? Ready, indeed. In the elevator, she told him of a slight change in plans. Zolac wanted dinner first. Stiletto said okay.

She took him to the penthouse suite where Heinrich Zolac, in a white tuxedo and holding a martini, greeted them with a smile. He gave Scott a hearty handshake. Zolac did not look like a terrorist. Medium-height, hair cut close to the scalp. No rings on his fingers.

Stiletto took in the large, high-ceilinged room, mostly white walls and furnishings, but he didn't linger on details. His focus was the dining table on the left side of the room, where Viktor Plotkin sat staring bullets at Scott. He made no effort to get up and say hello.

Zolac said, "I hope you don't mind a detour before we play, Mr. Cooper. I had some business to attend to and missed lunch." He led Stiletto and Elisa toward the table.

"Fine with me," Stiletto said.

Stiletto sat across from Plotkin. Zolac and Elisa sat at each end of the table.

"So you're looking for work," Zolac said.

"I'm looking at options," Stiletto said. A servant brought cocktails, and Stiletto took a sip of the martini. Perfectly mixed—and quite powerful—gin and vodka with a twist of lemon peel.

Elisa watched him with a gleam in her eye. Viktor fiddled with his silverware.

"Tell me about yourself," Zolac said.

"I'm not an idealist," Scott said. "I work for money, and go where the money is."

Plotkin finally looked up. Zolac's smile faded. "These two," Zolac gestured to his Russian companions, "have the same attitude about making money. Nobody fights for ideals anymore. Causes mean nothing. It's a shame. I still think the cause is worthwhile, but we need good people. We need experienced operators."

Stiletto drank his martini.

The servant who brought the drinks returned, book-ended by two others, and they placed salads in front of the four at the table. Zolac made small talk about his journalism days, focusing his attention on Stiletto while the two Russians sat and listened. Neither intruded on the conversation.

The servants carried in the dinner plates next, lamb cutlets, new potatoes dressed with oil, and green beans.

They ate quietly for a while, then Zolac spoke again.

"We are performing a needed humanitarian purpose."

"Which is?"

"Control."

"People?"

"Not controlling people in the traditional sense. Not keeping them in cages or having border guards face inward. I mean *giving* people control. Establishing order. Most people simply aren't equipped to handle the affairs of their own lives, so providing an environment where they are told what to do and when and how without the burden or stress of thought is what people like us can provide. That is the ultimate goal of our efforts. 'New World Revolutionary Front' is not just a name. It's a philosophy. A vision."

"It's much more ambitious than average," Stiletto commented.

"Exactly. And that is where our comrades have failed. They miss the greater importance of our cause."

"If the majority want control—"

"*Need* it. Deep down they are waiting for us to show them the way. I learned that when I worked for the progressive newspapers, the kind the conservatives rail against so much. The working class and the poor aren't stupid, but life is too hard for most of them. They need their trivial obsessions, their drink, drugs, and sports, to keep their mind off the agony of having to fend for themselves. And here I come bringing a solution, the hand that will feed in exchange for loyalty and a little of what they produce. I'm not asking much."

"What about those who might refuse?"

Zolac shrugged. "What do you think? There is a reason we need people like you."

AFTER THE servers cleared the dishes, Zolac led them to a corner table. Presently a table dealer with a poker set arrived from downstairs and sat at the head of the table. Zolac sat across from Stiletto while Elisa was to his left, Plotkin directly across from her.

They played for several hours, and in the end, Plotkin won the whole pot.

When the party finally broke up, Elisa escorted Stiletto back to his room. He stopped prior to opening his door and faced her.

"Nightcap?" he said.

"What do you have?"

"Vodka."

"I'd love a nightcap."

Once inside his room, she stood by the bed while he retrieved glasses from the bathroom. A bottle of vodka he'd purchased earlier sat on the dresser. He twisted off the cap and filled both glasses.

"Here's to crime."

They drank and sat at the table. Stiletto scooted his chair closer to her.

"Tell me," he said, "what are a couple of Russians are doing working for Zolac?"

She shrugged. "I'm ex-FSB. I didn't want to be a civilian with a normal job. What else am I going to do? My father cried when the Berlin Wall came down. He was a high-ranking member of the Party. He had a dream of being the supreme ruler of the United States one day. His dream became mine. But enough." She topped off her glass. "You know, you're boring."

"Really?"

"Plotkin found nothing interesting about you. It does suggest stability. No drugs or anything illicit, so if you are on the junk, you hide it well."

"I'm not a user."

"Good." She drank some more and refilled her glass. "Drink up, dear. Your vitamins are going to spoil."

Stiletto downed his glass, and Elisa poured more. They toasted again.

Presently they drained the bottle and Stiletto left the chair. While she talked more about her FSB days, he moved behind her and started massaging her neck and shoulders.

"Ooooh, magic fingers," she exclaimed.

"Tell me more about growing up in Russia."

She rose from the chair, setting down her glass and biting her lower lip as she reached for the zipper of Stiletto's pants.

"Why don't I," she said, "show you what I can do my fingers instead."

He didn't stop her.

PERFECT WEATHER for a picnic.

Kylie picked up a bucket of fried chicken and a few bottles of sparkling water. She and Moray drove to Civic Center Park located on Martin Luther King Jr. Way between Allston and Center Street. Within a stone's throw of the quiet park were city buildings and a high school.

Moray and Kylie spread out a blanket under a tree, and they sat to eat and look around. Car sounds from the street mingled with chirping birds, but it was still a serene setting. On the other side of the park, near the stone structure of the Berkeley Civic Center, a man stood holding a sign over his head and marching back and forth. Neither Kylie nor Moray could read the sign at this distance, but it was typical Berkeley. Somebody always protesting. Somebody always unhappy. Somebody always with an axe to grind against life in general and the powers that be in particular.

The greasy chicken quickly caused Kylie and Moray to run out of napkins, and they laughed as they searched through the used pile for a speck that wasn't already soiled. A few splashes of water from a nearby fountain cleaned their hands when they finished, and after returning the picnic gear to their car, they walked hand in hand like any other couple.

Except this couple was looking for a place to park a car bomb.

Moray wanted to try across the street near the police and court buildings. He figured the immediate streets around the park would be sealed off once the protest started, but the next street beyond, McKinley Avenue, might be a good place. They found the street lined with homes on one side and the backsides of the city buildings on the other. Street parking on both sides. Moray made some rough calculations regarding the blast radius and spread of the ZH4. McKinley would work; so would the next block over. Plenty of options.

Back at the house, while Moray sat to watch television, Kylie cracked open a can of cat food and went out to the front porch. She'd left food for the stray cat that morning, and noticed the dish under the front window had been licked clean. She scooped some more of the wet food into the dish. A pair of cat ears and cautious eyes peeked out from the bushes. Kylie squatted and called to the cat, but the animal didn't budge. She went back inside. After a moment, peering out the window, she saw the cat eating ravenously.

"Honey, come over here," Moray said.

Kylie put the cat food in the refrigerator and joined

Moray on the couch. Fox News was on the television. "What's happening?"

"She's one of us."

Kylie frowned at the young woman on the screen. Long dark hair, dark eyes, gold necklace, and a white blouse that was open a little farther down the front than Kylie would have worn. The woman's words were unmistakable as she told a talk show host about her discovery that the Central Intelligence Agency, despite policy changes ordered from the White House, was still engaged in the torture of terror suspects in the Middle East. But this time, they were using contractors to do the torturing. It was a way of keeping their hands clean.

"My sources are pretty clear about what's going on," the woman said. A graphic on the screen identified her as Sofia McKay, a freelance reporter.

"One team of contractors, for example," she continued, "has taken over a hotel in Saudi Arabia. They have the full cooperation of the Saudi authorities, and presumably CIA officials, and part of the ongoing interrogation includes hanging suspects from the ceiling by their feet."

The talk show host asked some questions, and Sofia McKay answered them. The conversation continued.

"Sounds like she knows what she's talking about," Kylie said, "but so what?"

"She's one of us," Moray said again.

"What does that mean?"

"She's part of the operation to keep the Americans off-balance while we carry out our mission. I'm sure she'll have something to do with phase two as well, but the goal is to put the Americans under a microscope so they'll be less likely to discover our activities."

"That sounds pretty flimsy."

"It isn't," Moray said. "Allegations of torture and mistreatment have been flying around since the so-called War on Terror started. Certain politicians sympathetic to our struggle will demand evidence and hearings and investigations."

"Does that mean we have people in Washington?"

"In the government, where it counts," Moray said. "They are waiting to play their part."

Kylie shook her head. "If you say so."

"It will only give us a slight edge," Moray said, "but that's all we need. We need them looking the wrong way for ten seconds. If that happens because they're busy proving they aren't water-boarding terror suspects, I'll take it. It will make the difference between success and failure and escape."

This time Kylie only nodded.

"McKay probably knows more than we do. That makes her a valuable prize indeed should she be found out and captured."

"So why put her on television?"

Moray laughed. "The government is not going to

grab a journalist off the street for questioning. No way. The firestorm that would follow would fill headlines for months. She's perfectly safe."

"You don't sound convinced."

"It's not a risk I would take," he admitted.

CHAPTER THIRTEEN

ZOLAC STOOD alone in his suite. The balcony doors were open, and ocean sounds drifted inside, but the pitch-black night hid the usual view. Only the sounds indicated the presence of the waves. Zolac poured a drink and stepped out onto the balcony. Everything was proceeding as planned. The report from Moray and Sarto in California, after their scouting mission, pleased him greatly. Other reports coming in from the guerilla squads massing in major US cities were also gratifying. Not much longer now, and the leader's plan would be full-speed ahead, the United States engulfed in fire.

The door opened behind him. Zolac turned to see one of his guards approaching.

"Plotkin is here, sir."

"For what?"

"He says he needs to speak to you about a problem."

"He can talk to Elisa. Remind him we have a chain of command here."

"He says he has spoken to her."

"And?"

"And now he needs to speak to you because he's convinced the American is a problem and she doesn't see it that way."

Zolac frowned. "Send him in."

The guard retreated.

Presently the bald Russian joined him on the balcony. The ocean rumbled in the distance. All they looked into was a black void of furious sound.

"Is something wrong, Viktor?"

The Russian outlined his concerns about Jake Cooper, the new man. "Elisa won't listen," he said. "I hope you will. We've come too far for somebody to derail us now."

"You have a point. For all we know, he's genuine but working for the Americans. You heard him. Whoever has the money has his loyalty. But he didn't go for the safe."

"We can't take the chance, Mr. Zolac."

Zolac sighed. He finished his drink but made a sour face. "I liked him. It's too bad, but I think you're right. Don't do it on the property. Get him on the boat, and make sure you're over deep water. No comebacks, Plotkin."

The Russian stifled a smile.

STILETTO KILLED time at the roulette wheel.

He didn't pay attention to what he won or lost but played steadily for several hours. His evening with Elisa Yanovna had been exciting, albeit certain body parts remained sore. He felt cemented in his relationship with the crew, but he hadn't heard a word from anybody since.

When Plotkin came up beside him and said, "We need to see you," Stiletto cashed in and followed the Russian across the casino. Finally, some action. Then two others joined them; none of the NWRF soldiers he had seen earlier, but a pair cut from the same mold. The security arrangements in the lobby prevented him from packing the Combat Government. Now he wished he'd found a way to circumvent those metal detectors. He had a feeling he'd need the gun.

Plotkin said they were taking Zolac's private elevator as he unlocked a door marked AUTHORIZED PERSONNEL ONLY and let Stiletto through. The troops followed and waited for Plotkin. Stiletto stopped and watched the Russian. Plotkin shut the door, and the automatic lock slammed home.

"Straight ahead," Plotkin said. The troops started walking. The elevator waited at the end of the bright hallway. The troops were almost there; Stiletto fell in step beside Plotkin as they neared the elevator.

"I didn't know Mr. Zolac had a private elevator."

"He doesn't," Plotkin said. He moved so fast Stiletto almost didn't block the Russian's right arm.

Plotkin pivoted, right hand close to his body, gripping a black stun gun. Stiletto brought his hands together, clamping them tightly against Plotkin's wrists. The flash of blue electricity snapped between the front prongs and singed Stiletto's shirt.

Scott sidestepped left, Plotkin's momentum continuing to carry him around. Stiletto kicked Plotkin in the stomach, and the Russian doubled over. Stiletto turned to face the onrushing troops, grabbing one by the wrist and wrenching a pistol out of his hand. The man's fingers cracked and he screamed, but Stiletto jumped back and raised the gun. He told the men to stop while he kicked Plotkin again.

They halted, the one with the broken fingers wincing as he raised his hands. The other lifted his as well, scowling at Scott.

Stiletto's aim didn't waver as he asked, "What's going on, Plotkin?"

"*Smyert spionam*," the Russian said, grunting as he rose. He repeated the words—"Death to spies"—and Stiletto saw the troops starting forward. He fired one shot from the captured pistol and the bullet hit Broken Fingers with a wet smack, but the man continued his lunge, and before Scott could move, the soldier's body collided with his. Scott landed hard on his back, the man's dead weight pinning him down. He stayed there and took aim at the remaining trooper, but the man kicked the gun from Stiletto's hand. Plotkin moved in with the taser. The bolt of blue electricity snapped to life, and when the prongs burned into his skin, Stiletto let out a cry. His body convulsed, and his vision went black.

STILETTO WOKE up and vomited on the deck of a large boat.

"How lovely," Plotkin remarked. He sat on a nearby metal box holding a short-barreled Kalashnikov AK-74U.

Stiletto's hands were tied behind his back. He scooted away from his mess, sliding easily on the floor of the deck. He moved closer to the wall and leaned against it.

They were well out to sea, the boat pitching up and down as it crested each wave. Salt tickled Stiletto's nose. His stomach turned over, but he didn't retch. Why did they have to put him on a boat? He looked over at the frothy waves slamming into the hull.

The surviving trooper from the hallway manned the helm behind glass in the elevated bridge.

"Why are you doing this, Plotkin?"

"You're a spy."

"I am not. You know who I am."

"I don't believe you. Elisa does. She thinks you're perfect. But I don't. I convinced Zolac, and here we are."

"What will you do when Elisa finds out?"

Plotkin shrugged.

"She'll be even more upset that you went over her head."

"Office politics. There are more important things to deal with."

"What would it take to change your mind?" Stiletto said. "To convince you?"

"Go back in time and show up six months from now."

Waves rocked the boat, and Stiletto groaned. Plotkin remained seated.

Stiletto felt for his belt and the hidden pocket where the razor blade waited.

"I can help with whatever you're doing. Even your boss said so."

"Right. By being dead."

The man at the helm cut the motor. The boat stopped but continued to undulate with the waves.

"And now we have reached the end," Plotkin said.

"You're going to shoot me?"

"Yes, now that we're out far enough that your body doesn't wash ashore and disturb the tourists."

Plotkin stood and raised the AK-74U. He approached Scott, who braced himself against the wall, his face defiant. Plotkin's eyes were eager as he lined up his sights. Scott pulled his legs back, then shot his feet forward. His heels hit Plotkin's left knee and the Russian screamed, staggering back and falling onto the deck as the boat crested another wave. Plotkin started yelling as he scrambled to his feet and the helmsman turned to look, and Stiletto sucked in a lungful of air and threw himself over the side into the cold water.

THE SHOCK quickened Stiletto's heartbeat and he wanted to open his mouth for more air, but instead pressed his lips together as hard as he could. He had the razor in hand and began sawing through the rope around his wrist as his body slowly sank.

Stiletto's descent started to slow, and now his wrists

were free. He let the ropes go and bent forward to slice at the ones around his ankles. His body started to rise. His lungs burned.

After the second set of ropes fell away, Stiletto twisted and aimed for the rear of Plotkin's boat.

STILETTO BROKE the surface, water splashing over his head.

The motor coughed and rumbled to life as he swam for the rear ladder. He pressed his lips together hard enough to hurt. He needed air, fast. Stiletto reached the boat, grabbed the rungs and pulled up enough to expose his head. He gasped, the rumbling motor covering him. Water splashed into his mouth, and he spat it out. Peeking over the side, he saw the troop back at the helm and Plotkin watching the water, his weapon at the ready, looking for any sign of life.

Stiletto swung his legs over the back and rushed Plotkin, the Russian turning as Stiletto landed a blow directly at his right kidney. The Russian started to yell, but Scott wrapped a hand over his mouth, clamping the other hand at the base of Plotkin's neck. One hard twist and the neck snapped. Stiletto let Plotkin fall, scooped up the AK-74U, and jumped back. The Russian landed on the deck with a thud, loud enough to make the man at the helm spin around.

The troop hauled out a pistol, but Stiletto already had a bead. He fired a burst that caused a bouquet of red roses to blossom across the troop's chest. He fell out of the bridge and landed hard on the deck.

Stiletto raced up the ladder to the helm and took control, panting as he steered for land. A cramp developed in his stomach, and he bent a little.

How to proceed now? He could go back to Elisa with righteous indignation, but if Plotkin had convinced Zolac, he truly had no standing. He had to report what he'd learned and see what General Ike wanted next, but he needed time as well, and a delay in the discovery of the bodies.

He found wallets on Plotkin and the other man that provided more than enough cash to get back to the hotel.

Once on land, he hailed a cab. He didn't explain why his clothes were still wet despite the driver's curious glance.

DIRECTOR OF Central Intelligence Carlton Webb had an enviable office with a window. The window looked out on one of the property's large parking lots, trees creating a thick carpet of green in the distance. Carlton Webb did not have an enviable job, however. No one person knew everything that went on at the Agency or the extent of its operations, but Webb knew enough. Such "privilege" brought burdens not everybody was equipped to handle, although Webb appeared to handle them just fine, having sat in the DCI chair through two administrations so far. In his mid-sixties with gray hair, his attention did not waver as Ike Fleming spoke.

"We don't know who this reporter is or where she's getting her information," the general said. "Her accusations are baseless. We are not torturing suspects. We are using enhanced interrogation techniques that are well within written policy, sir."

"I have no reason to doubt you," Webb said. "But the Senate Intelligence Committee wants to see us first thing in the morning." Webb paused for a moment. "This reporter, McKay, specifically mentioned Saudi Arabia. Has she talked about operations anywhere else?"

"Not yet."

"Then we don't have to show the committee anything other than what's going on in Saudi Arabia with the contractors. How long will it take to put the files together?"

"Rest of the day, part of the evening."

"I need you to put a crew together and get the material ready. Don't use anybody outside SAD or the Counter-Terrorist department."

"But those people are supporting current operations. If I pull from that group, it puts field personnel at risk."

"I know," Webb said. "Can we tell field ops to stand down for twenty-four hours? Forty-eight at the most?"

Fleming took a deep breath.

"We only have one chance at this, Ike," Webb said. "What we need is to put together enough information to refute the claims. We may not be able to do so publicly, but we need to show the committee the story isn't true. If we do not, you know the consequences. The committee can call for a formal investigation and threaten to withdraw covert funding. That would leave a lot more in the lurch than whatever your people are busy with. We can't accomplish the goal with just the legal team. If that means we put operations in a holding pattern for a day or two, that's what it means."

Fleming wanted to disagree further, but he held his tongue because the boss was right. He hated the idea. Stiletto was out there and so were others, each performing vital missions for the Agency in defense of the United States. They deserved every scrap of support home base could provide. He didn't want anybody feeling like they'd been left out to dry. If the worst happened and the Agency lost its funding, the consequences and effects of such a decision would do more than leave agents temporarily frustrated. Webb was right about that.

"What time is the meeting tomorrow?" the general asked.

"Nine a.m. sharp."

"We'll be there with enough to keep them from snooping too much, sir. Count on it."

The two shook hands and Fleming returned to his office, only to be intercepted by David McNeil.

"What now?"

"Stiletto called. Monte Carlo just went to hell, sir."

Fleming's head began to throb.

CHAPTER FOURTEEN

STILETTO SAT in his hotel room and waited.

After paying off the cab, he'd entered through a side door, telling the clerk at the front desk that he'd had a boating accident and lost his key card. The clerk issued him a new one. Taking the stairs to his floor, he found his room untouched, meaning the opposition had no reason to clean it out because they were waiting for Plotkin to return with a report of "mission accomplished."

Scott grabbed a mini-bottle of Johnny Walker from the corner refrigerator and a dirty bathroom glass and dug out his cigars. Sitting at the table with the drapes closed and his back to the wall, he smoked and sipped and kept the Colt in his lap.

He was halfway through the Cuban when the door lock beeped and clicked back.

Stiletto sprang from the chair with his gun in hand. Before Elisa Yanovna was fully through the doorway, she gasped and screamed. Stiletto grabbed a handful of her hair, pulling her inside and kicking the door shut. It closed with a loud bang. He dragged her a few feet to the bed and shoved her face down onto the mattress. She wore a simple white blouse and a dark skirt, one of her black heels slipping from a foot as her body settled on the bed. She flipped over, hands under her to shove off, but she froze at the unwavering mouth of the Colt's barrel pointed at her face.

"Surprise," Stiletto said.

Her words came out in a rush. "It wasn't my idea! Plotkin convinced Zolac, and they didn't talk to me!"

"Do you think I'm a spy?"

She shrank back, putting a little distance between herself and the cannon in Stiletto's fist.

"I don't know what to think."

"Where's Zolac?"

"Gone!"

"What's Zolac going to do with the ZH4?"

Her face reddened. "You *are* a spy!"

"Plotkin's dead, and you're next unless you tell me what I want to know."

"*Nyet!* Never! You'll never catch Heinrich! You'll never save your country from the fire we will rain down upon it! I'll die first!"

Stiletto tightened his grip on the gun. He didn't have time to soften her up. If Zolac had cleared out, he needed to find the man fast.

"Elisa?"

"What?"

"You'll die now."

Stiletto fired once.

Her white blouse turned red.

THE JAGUAR's engine rumbled as Stiletto powered away from the resort.

He held his cell to his right ear, and David McNeil answered.

"He's here, Scott. Hang on."

General Ike came on the line.

"Trouble?"

"You're the master of understatement, sir. What did David tell you?"

"That Monte Carlo went to hell."

"That's about right," Stiletto said and filled in the blanks. "Has Zolac shown up in Austria?"

"Not that our team has reported," the general said, "but I'll tell them to raid the place to see what they can find. Head for the embassy in Vienna and somebody will take you to the location."

"Who's the team leader on-site?"

"Mike Cutter."

"Perfect, sir. On my way."

Stiletto tossed the phone aside and shifted a gear. The Jag's engine howled as he rocketed down the open highway.

HEINRICH ZOLAC did not fly commercial. His status as second in command of the New World Revolutionary

Front gave him certain perks, and a private jet was one of them.

This particular jet was a luxury flying machine, the Bombardier Global 8000. Built to allow up to twenty travelers, for him alone, it was quite roomy.

Zolac sat in a soft leather chair beside a window with a drink in one hand and the phone in the other. The person he was talking to didn't Skype.

"Is it still safe to operate?" the man on the other end asked. He spoke in a low voice, almost gravely, and in the time Zolac had known the man, he had never raised that voice any higher. Konstantin Hristov, known throughout the European underworld as The Bulgarian, never needed to raise his voice. He was known to end lives with the snap of his fingers.

"I think we're fine," Zolac said. "Plotkin was simply overcautious."

"Have either Plotkin or Yanovna reported getting rid of the American?"

A chill raced up Zolac's neck. "No."

"Have you tried contacting them?"

"My concern was updating you and getting to the United States to link up with the team in Berkeley, so I haven't called them. I also haven't heard from anybody stating that removing the American did *not* go as planned. I trust our people."

The Bulgarian was silent for a moment.

"Have you spoken to the accountant about releasing

funds for the guerilla teams?"

"I emailed Gratien about it, yes."

"Terminate him."

"But why?"

"If the Americans are tracking you, if the worst has happened at the resort, if Plotkin was right, then the Americans may intercept the messages or somehow track you through Gratien. You will send two of our soldiers to Paris with orders to kill the man. Is that understood?"

Zolac swallowed a mouthful of scotch. One did not argue with Hristov. "Of course, sir."

"See to it immediately, Heinrich."

The line clicked in Zolac's ear. He lowered the phone. His hands were shaking, but two things were clear in his mind.

First, follow Hristov's instructions.

Second, contact Monte Carlo and confirm all was well.

As usual, Zolac reflected as he swallowed more of his drink, it was a mistake to make contact with the big boss and not be one-hundred-percent prepared. He would have been just as tough on one of his subordinates had the situation been different.

He just hoped he could call Hristov back with good news.

Because what if…

Zolac finished his drink and dialed Elisa Yanovna.

The jet's engine continued its dull throb inside the0 cabin.

IT WAS a twelve-hour drive to Vienna, and then a grind through stop-and-go morning commute traffic to the US Embassy at 16 Boltzmanngasse.

Stiletto exited the Jaguar feeling like a zombie. The resident CIA officer received him in the lobby, after which Stiletto showered and changed clothes and felt a little more human. The resident officer personally drove Scott to Zolac's hillside estate just outside Vienna via the A21, where they followed a winding road to the main gate. The CIA Tac Team had the entire property secured, the two agents at the gate only allowing Stiletto through when their team leader, Mike Cutter, personally vouched for Scott's identity.

As the resident officer drove away, Scott and Cutter shook hands.

"Long time," Stiletto said.

"Been having fun?"

"You wouldn't believe me if I told you."

Cutter started for the house, leading Stiletto along a stone path through a vibrant front yard full of colorful flowers, trees, and plant life. The low wall surrounding the property cut off all sight of the hills around the estate, and to Stiletto, that was a shame. He had become lost in the wonders of the view during the drive up, the green grass and blue sky, and the other homes dotting the landscape. But, of course, Zolac had his reasons, and probably tried to compensate with the vibrant front yard.

"We didn't have a lot of trouble breaching the gate,"

Cutter said. "There was only a token force here."

"So Zolac never showed?"

"Nope. But we have the next best thing."

Most of Cutter's troops were stationed outside, but some were inside, tearing the front rooms apart for information. It was Intelligence 101. There was always something to find. Cutter escorted Stiletto through the living room to an upstairs office where two of the tac team worked at a computer. It was a desktop machine on a desk in a corner, with the associated printer and other accessory machines off to the side.

Pictures sat atop the desk, Zolac and others Stiletto didn't recognize. Family pictures. It made Zolac seem almost human.

"Zolac's PC," Cutter said. "He's somewhere sending out e-mail messages, and the messages are being logged on this machine."

"Has he sent enough for us to pinpoint him?"

"Nope, but he was a little sloppy. He mentioned a name."

Cutter sorted through a stack of printouts beside the computer as the two tac team agents continued scouring the screen, printing pages now and then and transferring data to a separate hard drive connected to the back of the CPU.

"What did you find?" Stiletto said.

Cutter showed him a printed email. "Message to somebody named Felix Gratien in Paris. He's telling him to start wiring money to prearranged accounts. That's all there is."

Stiletto scanned the text of the message and agreed with Cutter. There were no other specifics from which they could work, but they had a name. Sometimes a name was all you needed to start unraveling the thread.

THE SENATE chamber held a silence not unlike that of a library.

General Ike sat next to DCI Webb at a wooden table on hard wooden chairs. Microphones sat before them, as did pitchers of water and very clean glasses. Both men had a stack of pages in front of them, notes on what they planned to testify to the committee about. Select members of their individual staffs sat behind the wooden gate at their backs, on call with briefcases full of more information.

Ahead of them was a raised dais where the members of the Senate Intelligence Committee would sit, high enough above the floor of the chamber to look down on Fleming and Webb, in what Fleming could only imagine was an intimidation trick. He'd sat in this chair before. He didn't have a lot of faith in the members of the committee, understanding the need for congressional oversight but not appreciating the fact that several members had used their positions to advocate for the dismantling of the CIA.

There were moments on the job when Fleming wanted to take a sledgehammer to the place himself, but not enough to see a major part of the United States' defense effort dissolved. Such a move would put the public at risk, the exact opposite of what Fleming, his boss, and agents like Stiletto wanted to happen.

As the fifteen members of the committee filed into the chamber and took their seats, Fleming, Webb, and the others in the room stood. After sitting down and calling the meeting to order, the committee chairman began, "Good morning, Mr. Webb and General Fleming."

The CIA men responded in kind, the microphones amplifying their voices in the chamber.

The chairman said, "I thought we were done discussing torture after the last time, but I suppose old habits are hard to break."

The chairman, Senator Leo Tattaglia from Vermont, was one of the committee members who hated the CIA's existence and wanted to make it go away. Fleming was glad he didn't have to answer. He let Webb handle that.

The Director of Central Intelligence, his folded hands resting on the stack of papers before him, remained cool.

"It's good to see you again, Senator Tattaglia. I can assure you that we are not having a repeat of last time."

"This committee will be the judge of that, Mr. Webb."

"Of course, sir."

Tattaglia referred to the committee's earlier hearing and investigation into the CIA torturing terrorist suspects in the early days of the War on Terror. Carlton Webb, newly installed at DCI at the time, had borne the brunt of the committee's wrath over altered and destroyed evidence, and the various attempts at deception on the part of CIA to keep the committee off the scent.

Fleming remembered the hearings well, but Webb had remained steadfastly supportive of his people the entire time. He, like Fleming, knew that a new kind of war required a new kind of fighting. While he was willing to admit that perhaps things had gone a little too far, giving a terror suspect a plate of cookies in exchange for information on mass-casualty-producing attacks wasn't realistic either—although he knew of one instance where cookies had indeed made a jihadist talk. Snickerdoodles, no less.

"We are here to determine," Tattaglia said, his voice booming through the chamber, "whether media reports of torture are true, and if the CIA is in violation of United States policy."

"I understand," Webb said.

"I don't believe you do, Mr. Webb."

Webb said nothing. His eyes remained fixed on Tattaglia.

"What do you have to say?" the senator from Vermont asked.

"The allegations are not true."

Tattaglia let out a noise that was half-snort and half-laugh. "On the contrary, we have reports from a young lady named Sofia McKay, who appears to have sources deep in the intelligence community, that say otherwise."

"Based on what, sir?"

"What do you mean?"

"Has Ms. McKay brought forth any evidence? Pictures, video, witness statements? I haven't seen any on television."

"You know how the media works, Mr. Webb. Sources remain confidential. The problem we have here is that you people have done this before. You're guilty until proven innocent."

Fleming, seated next to Webb, saw his boss stiffen a little. He tapped the table twice, their signal to "Watch it, pal," because the last thing either needed was an outburst in front of the committee to make matters worse.

"Although Ms. McKay has chosen not to produce any evidence of wrongdoing, and instead rely on hearsay," Webb said, "we have brought evidence to refute her claims."

"Please refute," Tattaglia said.

Webb and his staff set up a whiteboard and Webb began his presentation, showing pictures of holding cells in Saudi Arabia where contractors were carrying out their counter-terror and interrogation missions. Fleming joined him to explain in great detail several current missions and how captured combatants were being treated, reminding the committee of what policy currently allowed as "enhanced interrogation" and how his people in the field were following those procedures.

The presentation took about forty-five minutes, and a question-and-answer session involving the remaining members of the committee followed. The other members less hostile than Tattaglia, but Fleming, watching from his seat, wasn't sure they had everybody convinced.

When the Q&A ceased, Tattaglia took center stage once again.

"What you're saying is, Mr. Webb, is that Sofia McKay is a liar."

"Correct, sir."

Fleming stifled a grin.

"Why would she lie?"

"We know Ms. McKay is an advocate for certain causes that would give her an unfair bias to our work, sir."

"How do you know this? Are you spying on her?"

"We are not spying on her, sir."

"How do you know this?"

"She's on the internet if you would care to search."

Fleming tapped the table. Webb cleared his throat.

"I don't know if I like that tone, Mr. Webb."

"With all due respect, Senator, her information is readily available via a simple inquiry."

"She's doing this to get a better job somewhere?"

"I can't speak to her reasons, Senator."

"Uh-huh. Well. This committee will review your information in detail, and I don't know about the rest of my colleagues, but I'm going to recommend a full audit of your operations so we can see the material you've held back."

Webb pressed his lips together. Fleming took a deep breath.

Tattaglia looked up and down the row of committee members. "Do any of you have anything to add?"

Nobody did.

"This meeting is adjourned," Tattaglia said.

WHEN THE CIA jet landed at Orly airport in Paris, Stiletto cleared customs and smiled at the woman who waited for him.

He hadn't seen Marlise Delaby in a couple of years, and the sight of her warmed him inside. She was an agent for the Central Directorate of Interior Intelligence, the DGSI. A quick call from CIA HQ to French intelligence had arranged the liaison. The French, after a short briefing on the situation, had agreed to assist.

She returned Scott's smile. Her front teeth were a little crooked, and her glasses gave her a nerdy beauty Stiletto liked. She wore her long black hair tied back. Slim, with narrow hips and the biggest pair of brown eyes Stiletto had ever seen on a woman, those eyes lit up with her smile.

"Long time, Marlise."

"Don't I get a hug?"

He embraced her, and she returned the squeeze. She felt small in his arms. She always had. They had dated off and on when Stiletto was the CIA resident at the US Embassy in Paris after his wife Maddy died, but now only saw each other when business brought them together, like now.

When Scott held the embrace too long, she laughed

and shoved him away. They started walking.

"We have action in Paris?" she asked.

Stiletto gave her the rundown from the beginning, and as he spoke, the low mood he had felt on the flight from Austria began to lift.

"Who is Gratien?" she said.

"Zolac's accountant," Stiletto said. "The man in charge of the money, but still only a pawn in the organization. My job is to find him and make him talk. If he's moving money now, it means that whatever Zolac has in mind for the ZH4 nerve gas is starting to take shape."

"I need to call HQ."

Stiletto followed the French agent to her car, and she took him to a hotel where her office kept several rooms in reserve for temporary use.

"I figured you'd need some clothes," she said, "so I packed a case." She pointed to the bag on the bed. He told her thank you, opened it, and began sorting the clothes within, everything new and in the right sizes.

Marlise picked up the phone and checked in with her chief. She asked for information on Felix Gratien, the accountant. Stiletto sat at the writing table to check his gun and loaded magazines.

When Marlise finished her call, she joined him at the table. "We'll know everything about Gratien within the hour."

Stiletto loaded the last mag.

"Been a long couple of days," he said. "Though I did

spend them at a nice resort in Monte Carlo."

"You have all the fun. My office is choking me." She came over and sat on his lap, snaking her arms around his neck. "What shall we do while we wait?"

He hooked his right arm around her waist. Her body felt warm through her clothes.

"We can talk. When was the last time we had a nice long talk?"

She took off her glasses. "Do you really feel like talking?"

He didn't.

"THERE IS the high rise Gratien works in," Marlise said.

She and Stiletto walked along the sidewalk across the street from the building in question. They sipped coffee as they walked, anonymous souls blending with the rest of humanity.

"Which floor?"

"Twentieth. Quits every day at five p.m. sharp."

Stiletto checked his watch. Just after three. He asked, "What about his home?"

"Apartment's not too far from here."

Stiletto examined the building while tuning out the traffic noise. A wide boulevard separated his side of the street from the high rise. The building was a steel-and-glass structure similar to every other high rise in the world.

He watched two cars turn into the underground parking garage. Another vehicle, a white van, exited the garage and joined the traffic flow.

"Want to wait at his apartment?" Marlise said.

"No. Find out what kind of car he drives."

She took out her phone.

FELIX GRATIEN drove his gold Mercedes out of the underground garage.

Marlise, behind the wheel of a DGSI unmarked car, followed the accountant. In the thick boulevard traffic, it was easy to stay close yet avoid detection.

Ten minutes into the drive, Gratien stopped at a flower shop for roses, returned to his car, and resumed the drive.

Marlise said, "We have company. Green SUV."

Stiletto glanced back. The SUV tailgated their car, jerked into the left lane, and began to pass. Stiletto watched the passenger load a cut-down FN FAL and lower his window.

Stiletto let out a curse, powering down his own window and unbuckling his seat belt.

The SUV closed in on Gratien's Mercedes.

Stiletto scooted out the window to sit on the door frame with the Colt .45 in his right fist. The wind slammed into him, and he squinted as he aimed. The passenger in the SUV aimed his FAL carbine as Scott squeezed the trigger. The .45 slugs punched through the SUV, shattering glass. The SUV swerved, and the gunman pulled back.

As the gap between the Mercedes and the SUV grew, Marlise put her foot down and accelerated into it.

Stiletto rolled into the back seat, lowered the driver's side rear window, and took another shot, this time at one of the tires. He missed.

Marlise jerked her wheel and bumped Gratien's car. The frightened accountant had sped up too, but even the Mercedes could not outrun the modified government car. He slowed and tried to make a right turn off the boulevard, but he took the curve too fast. The rear end fishtailed and slammed into a light pole.

The SUV continued on. Marlise pulled in front of the Mercedes and, gun in hand, Stiletto raced out. He pulled a shaking and stunned Gratien from his car and coaxed him at gunpoint into the unmarked car. Gratien protested, but Stiletto batted him over the head with the Colt, ending further protest, and shoved him into the back seat.

"We're the only chance you have to live," Stiletto told the accountant, who looked at the CIA agent with glassy, semi-conscious eyes. Marlise drove away.

"Here they come again," she said.

"Lose them!"

Stiletto slapped Gratien awake as Marlise began weaving through traffic.

"Who are you?" the accountant said, squirming in the seat. "What's going on?"

"Heinrich Zolac."

"He's a client. What about him?"

"He's a terrorist, and we want to know where he is."

"That's crazy!"

"As crazy as the guys in the SUV who want to kill you?"

"You were the animal doing the shooting!"

Marlise shouted, "Scott!"

Stiletto fell atop Gratien and forced his head into the seat as the SUV roared close, the passenger firing his carbine. The back glass popped. Stiletto rose, bashed a hole in the back window, and fired twice in return.

Marlise sped through an intersection and caught an autoroute on-ramp. She increased speed.

Stiletto put his face close to Gratien's. "They're from your client! You've done your job, and now you're a loose end! Tell me where he is!"

"I don't know!"

"You know *something!*"

"He called me yesterday and told me to move money. It was nothing unusual!"

"His money?"

Gratien laughed. "You think you're after the big fish, but Zolac is just a cog in the machine!"

"Who does he work for?"

"A name you should know. Konstantin Hristov!"

The Bulgarian. The name flashed through Stiletto's mind seconds before gunfire drowned out his thoughts. Marlise swerved in and out of lanes, but the SUV stayed close.

Scott rose and fired out the back, cracking the SUV's windshield but missing the front tires. The .45 locked open, empty. Gratien made a move to escape. The accountant twisted and shoved Stiletto away, and Scott slammed against the door. Gratien opened the door on his side. Air rushed in and he tried to scramble out, but Scott cracked him over the head and pulled the door shut.

"My side!" Marlise shouted.

Stiletto moved across the seat while awkwardly slapping a new magazine into the Colt. The SUV's passenger fired at Marlise. Bullets shattered her window and she screamed, her hand slipping from the wheel. Stiletto fired back wildly, the Colt jumping in his hand as the car drifted across to the right shoulder, bouncing off the road and tumbling three times before landing on its wheels, the roof caved, both sides dented, and all glass shattered.

The SUV pulled off the road and reversed toward the government car.

Marlise didn't move. Blood covered the front of her clothes and the side of her head. Stiletto, woozy and bleeding, forced himself off the backseat. He crawled across the unconscious accountant, shoved open the door, and fell out into the dirt.

The SUV stopped, and the two NWRF gunmen jumped out. The passenger gripped his FAL carbine while the driver snapped back the bolt of a stubby MAC-10.

Stiletto coughed and crawled to the front of the car, braced the Colt on the fender, and fired once. The driver's head snapped back, a trail of blood following the bullet out the back of his head as he dropped. The passenger fired the FAL, Stiletto dropping back as the government car rocked with hits. Stiletto rolled into the open, firing the Colt as fast as he could. Each slug tore into the gunman's chest, ripping clothes and flesh apart in a wet mess. The gunman crumpled to the ground.

Stiletto held the pistol on the man a moment longer. The sirens screaming up the freeway announced the arrival of the cavalry.

He ran to Marlise, wiping blood from her face with his sleeve. Her eyes were closed, but he saw her chest moving with breath. The arriving paramedics pulled him away as he tried to unbuckle her seat belt.

"ARE YOU okay?" asked General Ike.

Stiletto spoke to his superior via secure cell in the hospital cafeteria. While the line was scrambled, he had to watch what he said because of the other ears nearby.

"I've been worse."

"And Marlise?"

"She's in bad shape."

"The accountant?"

"He'll live."

"Did he tell you anything?"

"He mentioned Konstantin Hristov. The Bulgarian."

Fleming grunted. "Certainly not an unfamiliar name, but is he involved with Zolac?"

"Gratien said that Zolac is part of the help. Hristov

is the man in charge."

Fleming was silent for a moment. "It explains a few things."

"Like what?"

The general explained how Sofia McKay's news report had sparked a meeting between him, the Director of Central Intelligence, and the CIA legal team with the Senate Intelligence Committee.

"It went well," Fleming said, "and we made our case that she is simply a muckraker trying to make a name for herself, but the usual suspect wants more information."

Stiletto suppressed a laugh. The usual suspect, indeed. The senator from Vermont, Leo Tattaglia, hated the CIA and wanted to see it gutted. He'd take any opportunity to create a problem for the Agency, its people, and its operations.

"Wouldn't it be interesting," Fleming continued, "as I've posited before, if Miss McKay is part of a counter-op using the media?"

"Might be a bit of a stretch, but I see what you mean."

"These hearings would serve the NWRF and a great many of our foes very well, especially if a prolonged investigation is ordered."

"What do you need from me now, sir?" Stiletto asked.

"Our primary goal must remain the recovery of the ZH4," Fleming said. "Hristov can wait."

"You want me to bring Gratien home for further questioning?"

"Yes, ASAP. Yesterday. However fast you can get here. I'll have our case officers in Paris go through Gratien's files. Maybe we can find something there."

"But, sir—"

"Do not wait even ten minutes, Scott. Marlise will understand."

Stiletto almost crushed his phone under a tightening grip. "Very well, General. See you soon."

Scott put the phone away. He wasn't going to leave until he knew Marlise would be okay. As he made his way to her room, he wondered if he was staying because he truly cared for her or if he trying to prove that he had not abandoned his family and caused his daughter to hate him.

The answer proved elusive, and he was probably afraid of it anyway.

STILETTO WAITED for over two hours, long enough for Marlise to clear surgery. Orderlies wheeled her bed into a recovery room, and Stiletto sat at her bedside watching her sleep. She was still under and he couldn't talk to her, but he held her hand for a while. Her skin was warm. He felt sick knowing he hadn't been fast enough to keep her from getting shot, but she would live to fight another day.

And that's what mattered.

CHAPTER FIFTEEN

AFTER STILETTO landed in the US, he turned Felix Gratien, the accountant, over to the interrogators and General Ike sent him home for forty-eight hours.

He dropped his house keys on the table inside the entry, hung up his jacket, and wandered into the kitchen, where the refrigerator revealed nothing but spoiled items. He tossed everything, then microwaved a can of chili and sat on the couch to eat.

Downstairs at his assigned parking slot, he unwrapped the bright red Trans Am and stuffed the cover in the back. Climbing behind the wheel, he started the engine and took a long drive. The concentration helped him unwind. The general wanted him to get some rest, but he didn't feel the least bit tired. He drove for ninety minutes before returning, and while reclining on the couch with a sitcom on TV, he dropped into a deep sleep.

STILETTO RETURNED to work promptly on the third day.

General Ike, in meetings with the DCI regarding the

continued Intelligence Committee hearings, was not available. Stiletto caught up on paperwork, then went out to the smoking deck. The deck was an outdoor sitting area between the middle floor and upper section of CIA headquarters.

Stiletto puffed on one of his Dominican Montecristos and drew in his sketchbook. Of all his regrets about his exit from Monte Carlo, the biggest was leaving behind the box of Cubans.

Presently, General Ike pulled up a stray chair and joined him.

"What's happening?" Stiletto said, tapping ash into a glass tray on the table.

"The Senate Intelligence Committee held their vote just now. They have decided *not* to go forward with a full inquiry into our activities overseas, which means the office won't be crawling with congressional auditors snooping through our files."

"But?"

"The usual suspect opposed to our existence has demanded more oversight because the accusation is just as bad as the truth, you know."

"He's been spouting that crap for years."

"Well, yours truly and the DCI will be making more trips to the Hill thanks to this *alleged* freelance reporter, Sofia McKay, and there may be a committee trip to Afghanistan to see first-hand what's happening there."

"You still think McKay is a plant?"

"I do. The damage wasn't what she thought it would be, but it created a problem we had to solve, and we may have taken our eyes off the ball. We just don't know how."

"It will be all over the media for a while, too."

"The day I start worrying about what CNN says regarding our work is when you should put me in a padded cell."

"Do we have anything else to talk about? Anything from a certain accountant?"

"Let's go back to my office. I think you'll be pleased."

Stiletto left his burning cigar behind and followed General Ike back into the building.

STILETTO AND the general stepped into a conference room with no windows. The bright fluorescent lights hummed. David McNeil sat at the circular table in front of a laptop connected wirelessly to the widescreen television monitor on the wall nearest the head of the table.

Stiletto helped himself to a glass of water from the pitcher in the center of the table, but the other two passed on his offer to pour for them. He sat down near McNeil, while Fleming remained on his feet looking at the screen.

"Let's see what you have, David," the general said.

McNeil tapped a few keys. The screen turned white, and then the names of cities in the US, larger ones, started appearing in two columns.

McNeil said, "Felix Gratien has told us a lot. The money transfers were in large amounts to various cities around the country. Those are the cities: New York, Los Angeles, Chicago, Denver, and others."

"What's the money for?" Stiletto said.

"He doesn't know. He was told to move the money, so he moved the money. But we ran a trace on anything that might be going on in those areas, and we found that they all have one thing in common."

McNeil tapped the keys again. The list of cities vanished, and what looked like a flyer announcing an event flashed on the center of the screen.

"This is all over the internet, and, turns out, all over the cities in question," McNeil said. "A group called Americans for Progressive Thought is organizing nationwide rallies. It's a coordinated effort that starts in two days. The only problem is that, in the past, these rallies have turned into riots. Lately, right-wing groups have been gathering in the same places to tell these people how wrong they are, and there's been violence, as I'm sure you'll recall."

"All over the news," Stiletto stated. "What are they mad about this time?"

"Same things they're always mad about," McNeil replied. "They want a government that the country didn't vote for, and they'll protest until they get it."

The general said, "That's enough, David. What's next?"

"A question. Why are Zolac and The Bulgarian funding this event? How does the ZH4 tie in, and what's the deal with the reporter?"

Stiletto drank some water.

"One of the cities is the target," Scott said, setting down his glass.

"Which one?" said the general. He turned from the screen to Scott. "And what if the rallies are a diversion and the ZH4 is to be set off somewhere we aren't looking?"

Stiletto shrugged. "Your guess is as good as mine."

"There was nothing in Zolac's Austrian place suggesting where the nerve gas would be used," the general said. He started pacing. "The accountant doesn't know. What other leads do we have?"

McNeil hit a few keys. The wall monitor cleared, and the face of Sofia McKay appeared in the center.

"The reporter," he said.

Fleming stopped, turning sharply to McNeil. "Seriously? You made a connection? We can't just go off my half-baked suspicions, David."

"Nothing half-baked about it, sir," McNeil said. "I've been digging into her background since she came to our attention."

McNeil hit a button and a video played on the screen. Sofia McKay, her dark hair tied back in a ponytail that swung back and forth as she moved hurriedly through a crowd, was shouting into a microphone as the crowd chanted around her.

"This is a rally in Austin, Texas six months ago," Mc-Neil said. He cut the sound and paused the video. A box appeared in the bottom left corner as he typed, a still picture filling the space. "There she is before the rally began with a fellow you might know, Scott."

"I don't recognize him." The picture showed Sofia McKay with an arm around a scruffy-faced man with dark hair.

"That's because when the two of you met," McNeil said, "you blew his face off."

Stiletto frowned. McNeil isolated the man's face and zoomed in on his neck. Stiletto lifted an eyebrow. He might not recognize the man's face, but he certainly recognized the neck tattoo.

"Darius Porter," Stiletto said.

"They seem rather chummy," McNeil remarked.

"Could be nothing," the general said. "If she was covering the event, why wouldn't she have crossed his path?"

"Multiple times, sir?" McNeil hit a button and more still pictures filled the screen. Different cities, different hairstyles and outfits, but each one showed Sofia McKay in the company of Darius Porter, and not just at the rallies. Two photos showed them behind a stage, sitting close together.

"Does she know he's dead?" Stiletto said.

"What do you think?"

"Probably not. What else do we have on her?"

"How about some aliases?" McNeil said. Passport photos replaced the event pictures, each one showing McKay's face but with a different name or nationality attached.

"See the last one?" McNeil said. "Sandra Dow. Wanted for attempted murder. She gets around, our Sofia."

"Do you think she'll know where the gas is being used?" the general said.

"It's worth asking," McNeil said. "She made a ruckus here in D.C. I can only imagine there isn't much else for her to do. Why not cover the rallies? Certainly fits her M.O."

"We can't just bring her in," Stiletto said. "Considering the scrutiny we're under, as well as the laws we'd be breaking—"

"I won't order it, of course," the general said. "But we need some way of getting into her head and finding out what she knows."

"What about her family, David?" Stiletto said.

McNeil sat back and folded his arms. "She has a sister in Ireland. Parents are dead."

Stiletto drank some more water.

The general stood facing both men with his hands in his pockets. McNeil looked at the general and at Stiletto, then back.

Nobody said a word.

They knew what needed to be done, but to speak it out loud would ruin the deniability the decision required.

SOFIA MCKAY, in a red one-piece swimsuit, climbed out of the pool. Dripping water, she grabbed a towel from a nearby chair and began vigorously drying herself in the morning chill. Her swim was a routine she'd followed for decades, and it always left her refreshed and ready for the day. She needed the comfort of the routine now more than ever.

Her mission to cause a major distraction at the CIA appeared to have worked, but some of the end results wouldn't see the light of day until Congress published the results of their investigation—if they did.

Her interview spots on CNN and Fox had certainly stoked the fire, creating a frenzy for the local talking heads to speculate about how the new administration might be diverging from the policies set by the previous president when it came to the interrogation of terrorists. She could only smile as she clicked through the tv stations in the evening. She had them all on the hook.

This afternoon she had another spot scheduled at CNN for a follow-up interview, with a new list of juicy allegations to keep the waters churning.

She showered and dressed in a classic blue suit and pearl earrings, tying back her long dark hair to look even more businesslike. Grabbing her car keys, she started for the front door. It was a large home outside DC, paid for by the NWRF, and so far nobody had decided to explore her background deeply enough to ask why an alleged freelance reporter could afford the rent by herself.

The last thing she did before opening the door was to check her purse for the pistol inside. Then she opened the door.

A man stood there, looming over her, and as she screamed, his right arm flashed toward her. The stun gun in his fist snapped and crackled, and as the tongs penetrated the fabric of her blouse and the electrodes touched skin, the scream, and all consciousness, stopped.

HER EYES snapped open, and she retched.

Some of her breakfast bubbled up onto her chin and dribbled down the front of her blouse. She couldn't otherwise move, her arms being tied around the back of a chair. She sat in front of a table in a small room with bare white walls.

She spat a few times, finally catching her breath, and let her head dangle above her chest. The spot on her stomach where the stun gun had made contact still hurt, as if somebody were pressing the lit end of a cigarette into her flesh.

The door opened, and a man entered. He wore street clothes, and as Sofia looked up at his face, she realized he was the man who had appeared on her doorstep.

He shut the door.

"Have a nice nap?" he asked.

STILETTO FIGURED saying "hello" would sound weak as he entered the interrogation room, but he wasn't expecting her reply to his quip either.

"Feels like college," Sofia McKay said. She sat up as best as her secured arms would allow. "I want water."

"Later."

"Hard case, aren't you?"

"No, just a poor working man."

Sofia remained still.

"Who are you?"

"Mr. Cooper to you. We are going to talk about a few things."

"You are not an official interrogator."

"You're right. That means you won't be water-boarded today."

"Tomorrow?"

"Maybe."

"So you're a commando. An assassin. CIA, right?"

"Depends on what day it is. You've met me on one of my routine office days."

"When do I meet the assassin?"

"Soon enough, unless you cooperate."

"Why should I?"

"Let's not make this hard, Sofia. I'll give you credit for knowing why you're here, but that's all the credit you're going to get." Stiletto pulled out the chair opposite Sofia and sat down. He placed a folder in front of him.

"Darius Porter is dead," he stated.

She blinked. "How do you know?"

"Because I shot him."

Her bottom lip quivered, and she took a deep breath.

"Where?"

"Iraq," Stiletto said. "He and two others were hijack-ing a canister of a nerve gas called ZH4. Know anything about that?"

"Do I?"

"Is Sofia McKay your real name?" Stiletto opened the folder and read from the first page. "We found so many. Sandra Dow. Melissa Furlberg. Carla Wilcox." He looked up. There was water in her eyes, but her face remained stoic. "Shall I go on?"

"No."

"You're not a real reporter. Who are you?"

"I'm not talking to you."

"Maybe I have something else that will persuade you."

He flipped a page in the folder, revealing three glossy black-and-white photos, which he placed in front of her. Sofia's eyes widened and she sat forward sharply, held in check by her tied arms. She let out a curse as she struggled, but then began to relax.

The photos showed a young woman going about her day. Loading groceries into the trunk of her car; watering flowers in the front yard, leaving an elementary school.

"Looks familiar, doesn't she?" Stiletto asked.

Sofia looked up with hot eyes.

"You're going to tell us what we want to know," Stiletto said, "or I'm flying to Ireland to shoot your sister."

"Not even you—"

"Oh, try me." Stiletto sat back with folded arms. "You'll be in a room like this till you die with a picture of your dead sis on the wall. I'll hang it myself."

Sofia didn't try to hide her rage. A red flush crawled up her neck.

"That's the problem with having a weakness, Sofia."

"And you don't?"

"I suppose I have one, but I forgot what it was."

If only.

Sofia examined the pictures some more, then closed her eyes. A tear trickled down her left cheek, pausing at the edge of her chin before dropping onto her blouse. It made no difference to the spit-up already there.

"All right," she agreed.

"All right, what?"

"I'll tell you. Don't hurt my sister. She isn't part of this."

"Now we're getting somewhere," Stiletto exclaimed.

He collected the pictures and returned them to the folder, producing another sheet of paper, which he placed in front of her.

"Plane ticket to Berkeley, California," he said. "We found it in your email. Your plane leaves tonight. Sorry you're going to miss it. What's happening there?"

She said nothing.

"Is that where the ZH4 will be used?"

"Yes," she said. She didn't make eye contact with him. "The target is Berkeley."

"When and where?"

"I don't know when."

"Do you know where?"

"Yes. There's a park. Civic Center Park. There will be

a protest there."

"We know about it."

"Right-wing counter-protests are expected," she continued. "When they show up, we'll wait until both sides start fighting, then release the gas."

"Why then?"

"We're going to blame it on the right wing."

Stiletto looked at her. Her body language showed total defeat. Using her sister as bait had been the perfect strategy.

"We have a full cover story prepared," she said. "It will start with me, then we'll send talking points to other contacts we have in the media and elsewhere, who will spread the story."

"What's the goal?"

"To create public resistance to conservatives in general and the White House in particular."

"Uh-huh. Everybody is going to argue more, and there will be more division and strife between those who don't vote the same way. That's not a particularly good endgame. What's the real plan?"

Nothing.

"Sofia?"

"Bring down the president."

"How?"

"Guerilla forces."

"Where?"

"Major cities. Strike-and-hide specialists from around the world."

"To do what?"

"Create chaos. Chaos will lead to the results we want."

"The president stepping down?"

"One way or another."

"If the president resigns, his VP takes over. The last time I checked, the man is just as right-wing as the president."

Sofia finally raised her head. There was a gleam in one eye.

"Are you sure?"

Stiletto felt a chill down his back.

"Who else is involved?"

"Some people in Congress."

"I need names."

"I don't know all the names."

"Think about your sister."

"*I don't know all the names*!" she repeated emphatically.

"Okay." Stiletto selected the pictures of Sofia's sister once again and spread them out on the table. "Keep her in mind anyway." He rose from the table.

"I'm telling you everything!" she shouted.

Stiletto shut the door behind him.

CHAPTER SIXTEEN

"WHY WOULD she know so much?" Fleming asked.

"If she's going to cover the events," Stiletto offered, "she has to be aware of the plans."

Fleming grunted.

They stood in a neighboring room with a tech at a computer station, watching Sofia McKay on a wall-length monitor. She had finally started to cry.

"She didn't know about Porter?" Fleming asked.

"Probably doesn't have any contact with home base," Scott replied. "She has her orders, and she's running on auto-pilot."

They weren't at CIA headquarters, but instead a black site facility in Virginia's Blue Ridge Mountains. The air inside the facility smelled funny. Fresh air was pumped in from vents on the surface, but by the time it reached them, it wasn't entirely fresh anymore.

Fleming addressed the technician. The PC monitor showed an almost x-ray outline of Sofia McKay's body. Certain portions of her body were red, others blue.

"Has she shown any deception?" Fleming said.

"None at all, sir," the technician said. "I would say she's indeed telling the truth. Her brain pattern showed the opposite before she saw the pictures of her sister."

"What did the pattern show?"

"Deception," the technician said. "Or the thought-pattern related to it, I should say," he added. "In other words, she was working on a lie until she saw the pics."

Fleming nodded. To Stiletto, "What do you think?"

"I think I should get on a plane to Berkeley."

"Not our jurisdiction," the general said. "From this point, we need to hand it over to the FBI."

"They could use a consultant. Somebody familiar with the case from the opposite end."

Fleming didn't reply right away.

"My buddy Toby O'Brien works out there," Stiletto said. "Special agent. He and I can work together on this."

Fleming finally nodded. "Go back and find out who's in Berkeley. The operatives' names."

Stiletto returned to the interrogation room, and Sofia looked up sharply. If her tears embarrassed her, she gave no indication.

"Names. The people in Berkeley."

"Robert Moray and Kylie Sarto," she said. "Darius was supposed to be there too. They'll have replaced him, most likely."

Stiletto left the room again.

"What do we do with her, General?"

Fleming watched the woman some more.

"It's a problem."

"If she vanishes completely, the media will start asking questions."

"We can't let her out and tell her to keep up the deception. If her goal is to disrupt our operations, telling this story will indeed do that."

"We keep her here?"

"Let the media say whatever they want," the general said. "It's never stopped them before. She has more information that we need to get out of her. The accountant, too. Between the two of them, we can wrap up their whole organization."

"Do you have a sense of irony about this situation, sir?"

Fleming turned to Stiletto with a half-grin. "I do, indeed." Fleming started for the door and Stiletto followed. "Let's call the office and get you squared away for Berkeley. Maybe you can take McKay's place on today's outgoing flight."

Stiletto didn't hide his smile.

DURING THE ride to headquarters in the back of a black sedan, Fleming called McNeil at the office and told him to run a check on the names Robert Moray and Kylie Sarto.

When Fleming ended the call, Stiletto, seated next to him, said, "There's something we haven't talked about, General."

"I know."

"What do we do? Her claim that the vice president is working with the NWRF is pretty outrageous."

"But not unrealistic, I'm afraid," the general said. "It's the Bulgarian. He's not only an international criminal, but he's also using his money to influence elections all over the world through bribery, collusion, or blackmail. Who knows which of those got the VP under his control?"

"The President will want proof, and maybe harder evidence than McKay can provide."

"We'll see what's on her computer and hidden in that expensive home of hers," Fleming replied. "But leave that one to me. I'll tell the director, and he can brief the President at his discretion."

Fleming and Stiletto returned to the SAD offices in the bowels of the headquarters building, where McNeil had a work-up on both Moray and Sarto. Stiletto, having only seen their faces through a night scope, and during combat as well, could not positively say they were the pair he had tangled with in Iraq, but he looked forward to facing them in the daylight—before their plan came to fruition.

Fleming passed the word to the FBI, who said Stiletto was welcome to consult with their field agents in Berkeley, but time was running out.

The rally was less than twenty-four hours from taking place.

They had to work fast.

HEINRICH ZOLAC, having joined Moray and Kylie in Berkeley, paced the living room. He had just ended a call with Hristov that had contained nothing but bad news.

From the time he had left Monte Carlo to the remaining hours leading up to the Main Strike, a lot of the carefully structured organization of the New World Revolutionary Front had come unraveled.

Felix Gratien—alive and in US custody.

The boss, Hristov, aka the Bulgarian, had phoned with the news, and the leader was not happy. They were losing too much. First Yanovna and Plotkin, then the raid at Zolac's Austrian home, and now the accountant.

There wasn't much Zolac could do from where he was, and he had to admit that there wouldn't be much he could do even if he had been elsewhere. He had, at first, easily shrugged off American involvement in the recovery of the ZH4 in Iraq. Now, he realized, he should have taken it more seriously and alerted the organization instead of trusting that the rapid forward pace of the plan would render interference moot because there was no way the Americans could stop them in time.

He still didn't think they could stop him.

But surviving the day was now in doubt. They might not stop him, but they could catch him before he escaped. He didn't plan on allowing them to take him alive.

Zolac cleared his throat and straightened. He did not want Moray and Sarto to see any lack of confidence, but they had a right to know about the sudden complications,

even though they, for sure, wouldn't survive the day. He'd
see to that. It was his primary mission, after all, and the
reason he'd flown out here. Had Porter not been killed,
he'd have carried out the removal of the two loose ends
before meeting his own demise at a later date.

The murders didn't bother Zolac. They would not lack
for volunteers already in the organization or fail to recruit
outside the circle when Hristov conceived the next operation.

Zolac returned to the adjoining room, where Moray
and Sarto were examining a street map spread out on the
kitchen table. There were marks on the map correspond-
ing with closed streets and locations where police were
telling owners to move their cars or having them towed.
Social media provided much of that information, the posted photographs mostly the effort of organizers already
in the area. Whether they knew who they were helping,
Zolac didn't know.

After some discussion, they decided their best bet with
the car bomb was to park it a block away from the spot
they had originally intended, on Grant Street instead of
McKinley Avenue. The proximity of the city buildings
to McKinley made it impossible to park a car there. The
whole street was being cleared. The authorities wanted
nothing near those buildings.

The car bomb had been easy to assemble, with parts
available at most hardware stores and others fabricated
for the project at a nearby "makers studio" where power

tools and other machining-related implements were available like books in a library.

The ZH4 cylinder, mated to a carrier made of two two-by-fours and a plank, sat in the back seat of the rental car, wired with a timer, and, most importantly, an explosive on the release valve. The rest of the car was wired with C4, too. The explosive force would rupture the cylinder and release the ZH4, and cause a great deal of damage to the vehicles immediate environment.

Throughout the evening, the trio put the plan in final form and waited for the next day. Zolac told them that he had a plane on standby to take them away as soon as they parked the car and started the timer.

He didn't tell them that he planned to be the only passenger.

FLEMING HAD been joking about taking Sofia McKay's place on her flight to Berkeley. He'd instead arranged for one of the Agency's private jets to ferry Stiletto across the country. The jet landed at Oakland International, stopping in front of an empty hangar, and when Stiletto started down the steps to the tarmac, he didn't hide his smile.

His longtime pal and current FBI Special Agent Toby O'Brien waited beside a black government car wearing a chauffeur's hat. It clashed with his G-man suit.

Stiletto approached O'Brien with an outstretched hand as wind hammered across the runway.

"Where's the rest of the uniform?" Scott asked.

O'Brien laughed and tossed the hat in the back seat of the car. "Come on, there's a lot to go over."

Stiletto stowed his carryon in the back seat of the Chevrolet and joined O'Brien inside. The car was stripped of everything but necessities, which meant no CD player. O'Brien, a country music aficionado, probably hated that more than Scott did. He, of course, preferred jazz to country.

"What's new?" O'Brien asked as he drove away from the parked jet and headed for an automatic gate between two hangars.

Stiletto gave him an update on his life and received one in return. O'Brien's family was doing well. Scott felt a twinge of hurt at the description, but he knew O'Brien didn't talk about his kids with any malice toward Stiletto. It was a fact of life he had to live with. Other people had intact families. He didn't, but that did not make him less of a person, nor did it make O'Brien better than him.

At least, that was what Stiletto told himself. It was hard not to believe otherwise.

"Still on the Bureau's softball team?" Scott asked.

"Yup," O'Brien said. He passed through the automatic gate and turned onto the road. "We take on the DEA in a couple of weeks. They won last time."

Stiletto and O'Brien had met back in basic training in the Army, both taking separate MOS specialties but ultimately reconnecting at the JFK Special Warfare Center, where they forged a strong friendship as their duties sent them around the world. O'Brien had offered to help

Stiletto join the FBI after Maddy died, but Scott had preferred CIA. He had felt at the time that life as a special agent wouldn't be busy enough to keep his mind of the things he didn't want to think about.

O'Brien powered the government car up a freeway on-ramp to Interstate 880 north. Traffic was thick, and O'Brien started to slow down.

"What's the layout?" Stiletto inquired.

O'Brien laughed. "We're trying not to panic."

"That's a good start."

"We asked the governor straight out to activate the National Guard and bring in their Nuclear, Biological, and Chemical warfare equipment, and he refused until my boss called Washington and somehow got the director to talk to the President, who called the governor. Now the Guard is on the way."

"Has anybody asked Berkeley to cancel the rally?"

O'Brien laughed. "That went well. The city thinks the big bad government is trying to stifle their expression, so no, the rally will go on as scheduled."

"Probably wouldn't make a difference anyway."

"We have medical crews standing by," O'Brien continued, "and the plan right now is to keep everything outside the view of the plaza until they're needed. Hopefully they won't be, because we don't want to scare anybody."

Stiletto said nothing. Traffic slowed some more, as a semi kept Scott from seeing how far up the road the delay continued.

"Do you have any idea what we're looking for?"

"Nope," Stiletto said.

"But it's for sure a chemical attack."

"Yup."

"Car bomb? Aerosol dispersal?"

"I have no idea, Toby. All I know is what our suspects look like."

"And if they've planted the bomb and left town?"

"Toby, I don't have any answers for you."

O'Brien let out a breath. "I get it."

"I honestly feel powerless. We know something is going to happen, but we don't know where or how to stop it."

"We'll have to get lucky."

"I don't believe in luck."

"What *do* you believe in?"

"An intense, focused search of the target area," Stiletto said. "With the Guard's NBC gear, we should be able to detect the ZH4 before it's used."

"And if we don't?"

"Then the morgue is going to get very crowded."

Both men stopped talking as the grim reality settled upon them. O'Brien continued the slow drive through traffic.

"GOOD LUCK," Zolac had said.

Followed by, "I'll be waiting with the car. When you return, we'll head for the plane I have standing by."

Moray didn't believe a word the man said.

He drove the rental with the wired-to-explode ZH4 canister in the back seat, a blanket covering the kit. Moray's palms were sweaty, and a nervous knot refused to leave his stomach. With every bump, he thought the bomb might go off. From a technical and engineering standpoint, he knew that was impossible. From an emotional standpoint, he felt it very possible indeed.

The heavy traffic downtown made the going very slow, but that was the result of the street closures around Civic Center Park. With the windows down, Moray already heard the beginnings of the rally: somebody on a loudspeaker leading a chant, and the noticeable heavy police presence even away from the park. The police weren't simply riding in cars. Some were mounted on horses and were traveling along the side of the road as the cars squeezed by.

Moray checked his rearview mirror. Kylie wasn't directly behind him anymore, but he knew she was back there.

Prior to leaving the house, they had shared a guarded chat. Kyle was seemingly concerned about the disappearance of the cat she'd been feeding, the feline having been gone for two days now, but Moray assured her that the animal would find its way back. Then they lowered their voices and spoke about what to do upon their return. Both were armed, the Beretta Model 92s once again tucked into shoulder leather, fully loaded. Moray had no intention of dying today. If Zolac planned to leave alone, they had a surprise in store.

Presently Moray turned onto Grant Street and cursed. Residents in the areas closed to traffic had moved their cars to this street, and every curb space seemed full. It wasn't until he reached the end that he found a spot to put the rental. Executing one of the most tedious and careful parallel parking maneuvers he had ever attempted, he put the rental squarely between an ancient VW Bug and a Honda that had seen better days.

A car pulled up directly beside him.

Kylie.

She smiled.

Moray turned off the rental and reached into the back seat, flipping the blanket up enough to reach the timer. It had been pre-set for two hours. He pressed a button, and the countdown began. He recovered the bomb, stepped out of the rental, and climbed into the passenger seat of Kylie's car. She drove off.

He let out a deep breath.

"Bet you're glad to be out of that car," Kylie said.

"You better believe it."

Kylie turned at the next corner and merged into the heavy traffic once again.

Now to deal with Zolac.

ZOLAC, ALONE in the house, paced the floor with his cell phone to his ear.

The Bulgarian was on the line.

Again.

And the news kept getting worse.

"Sofia McKay has disappeared," the leader told him.

"How?"

"We're not sure. She missed a CNN interview, and I sent word to one of our operatives in the area to check on her. He found the door to her house unlocked and Sofia gone."

"Any sign of a struggle? Something to suggest she'd been taken?"

"All appeared normal, except for the purse and car keys she left behind."

"She didn't go willingly, then."

"I don't think so," Hristov replied. "Have Moray and Sarto departed with the bomb?"

"Yes." Zolac checked his watch. "They should have placed it by now."

"I do not think the McKay problem will affect the plan."

"Certainly not," Zolac said. "Even if she tells them everything, they won't be able to stop us in time."

"My instructions have not changed, but I have sent word to the team leaders to be extra vigilant. Once they get started, the plan should follow its natural course."

"Absolutely," Zolac agreed. At least he hoped so. He dared not voice the opinion, however. He added, "And if we start the guerilla campaign a little sooner, it may help some of the teams accomplish their goals and escape before the authorities can catch up."

"I've already advised them to relocate, but you have a point. I will add the order."

"I have to go," Zolac said.

"Have they returned?"

"Yes."

Hristov hung up without saying good-bye. Zolac jammed the phone in a back pocket and pulled a silenced pistol from a holster on his belt. He gave the suppressor a reassuring twist before taking a seat on the couch.

KYLIE SHUT off the car.

Moray stepped out first, giving Kylie a curt nod, and headed for the front door with his keys in his left hand. Kylie left the car and hopped smoothly over the side gate to go around to the back door.

Moray jiggled the keys as he approached the porch, let them fall, and bent down to pick them up. A quick motion off to the right, and he looked over in time to see the rear end of Kylie's cat sliding under the porch, its tail swaying briefly until it too disappeared from sight. Moray smiled. At least *it* was safe. He wasn't a big animal lover, but Kylie's attachment to the cat was enough to make him tolerate the attention she provided.

Moray rose, slipped the key into the lock, and turned. He drew the Beretta 92 autoloader from under his arm and held it close to his leg.

The front room was clear. He heard the television, the volume low.

Moray shut the door and proceeded into the living room. Zolac was on the couch.

"Mission accomplished," Moray announced from the archway between the rooms.

Zolac looked at him and frowned. "Where's Kylie?"

"She isn't here?"

Zolac rose, not bothering to hide his weapon as he began to bring it up.

"We've had enough trouble, Moray."

"Look behind you."

Zolac blinked, hesitating, then turned his head. Kylie stood in the other archway between the living room and kitchen, covering Zolac with the snout of her Beretta. She did not blink, and the pistol did not waver in her two-handed grip.

Moray raised his gun, and Zolac turned sharply to him.

"Put it down, Heinrich."

Zolac's gun clattered to the floor.

"Was the plan to shoot us and go? Let the Americans find us?"

Zolac replied, "Something like that."

"Is there really a plane waiting for us?"

"It's waiting for me."

"Not anymore."

Moray fired twice, and Kylie fired three times. The rapid snaps echoed loudly in the confined space, but each bullet hit where it was aimed, Zolac's torso exploding in bursts of red that splattered the floor and the couch. Zolac hit the floor hard and didn't move again, the pool of red below him growing as his life left him.

Kylie went to the body, and a quick frisk revealed Zolac's cell.

Moray held out a hand to her.

"Come on!"

She ran to him and they hustled out of the house, back into the car, and away.

MORAY DROVE with his hands tight on the wheel.

"His last call was to Hristov," Kylie reported as she examined Zolac's phone. "Do we call now?"

"Let's get to the jet first," Moray said, driving down Eastbound 80 with the ocean off to their right and the sweeping span of the Bay Bridge growing in the distance. "Once we get on the jet, we can call, and he'll tell us where to go."

"What if he—"

"He might," Moray agreed. "But if we don't try to get back in the fold, we'll be marked for life, however long or short that may be."

Kylie sucked in a deep breath. She looked at the passing scenery.

"I don't like the idea of life on the run," she told him.

"Get used to it. One way or another, we'll be on the run, either from our people or the US government."

Kylie said nothing more.

CHAPTER SEVENTEEN

PATROLMAN PETER Brick stayed close to the two National Guardsman as they started walking along Grant Street carrying their NBC detection device.

Brick was a twenty-five-year veteran of the Berkeley police force, and it showed on his face. He had a line or wrinkle for every year, every bust, every grim discovery of a body in an alley. The worst part about being a Berkeley cop was the city administration and the sycophants in police management. They favored the crooks at the expense of the citizens and had arbitrarily decided that certain laws didn't apply on certain days. If he was with the cadre overseeing the protest, he'd have been ordered not to interfere if anybody started destroying property, or even fighting. The town would maintain its penchant for free speech and rebellion even if the whole city burned down in the process. If taking a job farther south in San Jose or going north to Contra Costa County wouldn't have affected his pension, he'd have skipped town years ago.

He rode atop a horse as the two Guardsman carried out their duties. One held a clipboard, noting vehicle makes and license plates, while the other carried a contraption Brick only had a cursory knowledge of from his brief chat with the two soldiers. They were using what they called a JCAD, or Joint Chemical Agent Detector, which could determine whether any of the vehicles contained a chemical weapon. It looked like a Geiger counter and might have been based on the same concept. The three men and the horse methodically worked their way from car to car, the guardsman with the JCAD moving the wand from one end of each vehicle to the other before moving onto the next.

Brick listened to the radio chatter from the Motorola unit clipped to his uniform shirt. None of the radio calls were urgent, but cops stationed around the block of Civic Center Park called for extra cops for various incidents they were witnessing, and Brick had to wonder why. They didn't have authorization to stop anybody. They were supposed to let the radicals blow off steam, and judging by the noise and chanting, they had steam to spare. Brick didn't have to work hard to imagine the waving signs upon which protest slogans and obscene words had been scrawled. These kids hated the new President, and they weren't afraid to shout it out loud.

Counter-protestors were expected, but none had arrived yet. Brick was beginning to think the rumors of a clash had been blown out of proportion. What he knew for sure was that the Feds had high confidence of a chemical bomb attack, and that weighed on Brick's mind more than anything.

The guardsmen checked off another car and moved to the next.

They weren't the only team checking cars. Other two-man units and their police escorts were working nearby streets as well. Nobody knew if the chemical weapon had been placed in a car and rigged to explode or not, but the Feds thought it was a possibility, so they had the beat cops checking cars while they presumably were doing their own work. Brick's rank wasn't high enough to find out what the FBI was actually doing, but they had a command tent set up out of view of Civic Center Park, so he figured they were working as hard as everybody else.

On to the next car…

It was hard not to be cynical, Brick thought as he urged his horse forward, the animal's metal shoes clomping on the asphalt beneath them. There had been so many terror warnings, drills, and false alarms over the last two decades that Brick wondered if it was all somebody's idea of fun. Raise the alarm, rush out the troops and emergency crews, spend some of the city's and government's money, and have a few laughs.

And the next car.

The JCAD equipment didn't click and clatter the way a Geiger counter did when the device detected radiation, but the guardsman with the gear apparently trusted his system to scream or beep if it found something.

It was a nice day out, only a few scattered clouds in the blue sky, and if all Brick did was ride a horse in such weather and didn't have to swing his nightstick against the skulls of the hippies up the block, so much the better. He'd get some juicy overtime for sure. They always did when the protestors came out to play.

The guardsman approached another car, this one a gray Nissan sedan parked a little askew. They started at the front bumper. The guardsman with the JCAD slowly moved the wand from the front to the fender and along the side. Brick spurred his horse closer because of what he saw in the back seat. There had been plenty of miscellaneous crap in the other cars, but the blanket in the Nissan was different.

Nothing indicated what was under the blanket, but the object looked long and cylindrical. Brick keyed his Motorolla and called for the Feds to assist as the JCAD wand passed over the back area and started beeping. The guardsman let out a string of curses and stepped away, Brick moving his horse back as well. The animal had sensed the change in attitude and was becoming a little upset. Brick had calmed the horse and moved the animal farther away when a large truck turned up the street. The guardsman waved.

The bomb disposal unit. It was a huge two-ton truck on really big tires, and it had a diesel motor that was loud enough to drown out the protesting from Civic Center Park.

Brick decided it was best for him to keep his distance as the truck pulled alongside the Nissan. Had they really found something? Had they saved the day? A smile tugged at the corners of Brick's mouth. Boring shift, yeah, but maybe—

IF THERE was a time when the odds were stacked against them, Stiletto knew this was that time.

He stood in the back of the FBI's command tent near the protest area, drinking a cup of tea and feeling like a useless limb. The Feds around him, led by Toby O'Brien, had the situation under as much control as possible.

Search teams were checking cars, using equipment from the National Guard. Stiletto wasn't up to date on the latest tech, but the teams would be, and that was what mattered. The men using the gear knew how it worked.

Medical personnel were standing by. During the briefing earlier in the morning, the medical crew had shown the Feds their containment area, where they hoped to corral as many people as possible should an "incident" take place. They had an antidote for the ZH4, it turned out, but not enough for everybody. Stiletto, O'Brien, and the Feds had all had doses of antidote injected into their bloodstreams, but it was no guarantee. While they could plan for a standard sarin gas attack, the ZH4 was the same but different, so nobody knew if the antidote would work against this particular mutation.

A table full of monitors occupied Scott's attention, where cameras were focused on various spots around the protest area, but nothing out of the ordinary had caught his or anyone else's attention. A lot of people, a lot of signs, a lot of noise, and a lot of anger—the main components of the modern protest.

The ground shook.

"What the hell?" O'Brien said, detaching from the agents he'd been speaking with and running to the monitors. He touched a panel that allowed him to change the screenshots, but none of the views he cycled through revealed where the blast had originated.

A chill raced up Stiletto's spine. They attack had just taken place, and all he could do was stand there.

Alarms blared, the alert system the National Guard had set up around the area. There was chemical residue in the air. No doubt about it now.

Stiletto grabbed Toby and they ran out of the tent, looking left, then right.

"There!" O'Brien said, pointing.

A cloud of gray smoke climbed skyward from behind the city buildings across the street. The wind was blowing the cloud their way.

There would be casualties.

If Sofia McKay had been telling the truth, the chemical attack would signal the guerilla forces within the US to begin their attacks, too.

They were going to have their hands full.

CHAOS REIGNED.

Federal agents, cops, and National Guard troops immediately pulled on gas masks and headed for the crowd of protestors. Loudspeaker announcements told of the chemical weapon attack, and that everybody exposed had to proceed to medical containment areas.

The crowd panicked, turning from a mass of individuals clustered in one area to a mass of frightened rats running every which way.

When some of them started dropping, the panic reached uncontrollable levels.

While bodies thrashed on the ground, cops moved on those still on their feet, herding them toward the containment tents. They clashed violently with some, who quickly succumbed to the poison in the air. The medical crews rushed in as well, but it was quickly apparent that they were overwhelmed. It didn't help that those on the ground had no chance of survival.

Worse, the toxic cloud of ZH4 nerve gas was spreading over the city, propelled by an uncontrollable wind from the bay. People not even near the epicenter would fall victim to something they didn't understand and couldn't combat.

"IT DOESN'T look good, Scott."

"No kidding," Stiletto snapped.

He leaned against a wall at Alta Bates Summit Medical Center. There was no quiet place to talk on the phone, but it would have to do. The noise inside the building was enough to make a man deaf, or at least prevent him from thinking clearly. Casualties so far were huge, and the number was growing.

"We're watching the news," Fleming said, "and it looks like it's spreading throughout the city."

"It'll go beyond Berkeley and into the East Bay hills before nightfall," Stiletto said. "We're at the mercy of the wind," he added.

"Are you safe?"

"Gas mask and antidote, so for now, yes."

"Any leads?"

"O'Brien says the guard troops who found the car radioed the license plate a few seconds before the explosion, so we're checking on that. Maybe it will give us something."

"We'll be monitoring the airports," Fleming said. "Moray's, Sarto's, and Zolac's faces and descriptions have been sent to Homeland Security, so if any camera catches them, we'll know where they are."

"Won't be that easy, General. They may be out of the country already."

"We don't have much else, Scott."

"That's what makes me so mad, sir. I'll be in touch."

Stiletto ended the call and went to find O'Brien.

TOBY O'BRIEN strained the government car's engine as he barreled through traffic, Stiletto in the passenger seat beside him and two more FBI agents in the back.

The Nissan was a rental car, the license plate registered to a local Enterprise office.

They found the office deserted and the doors unlocked.

The staff had apparently fled the area, which was good, and Stiletto went behind the counter to type the license plate number into a computer. The address the renters had provided appeared on screen, and the crew piled back into the car.

O'Brien stopped the car in front of the house that had been used by Moray and Sarto. The agents emerged with drawn guns, but Stiletto kept the Colt holstered as he followed the team. O'Brien kicked in the front door, and they ran inside. It wasn't the best way to enter a potentially hostile environment, but even Stiletto had to admit they were running out of time.

They found Zolac's body right away. Stiletto examined the dead man's face.

"Ringleader," he announced.

"How do you know?" O'Brien asked.

"Because I played poker with him a few nights ago."

The agents searched the house while Stiletto went to the kitchen and called General Ike.

"Very odd development," Fleming said.

"Not really," Stiletto replied. "Zolac wasn't here to help them get away, he was here to punch their tickets. Obviously, he wasn't fast enough on the draw."

"How long has he been there?"

"Rigor hasn't set in, so not very long. That means Moray and Sarto may be still in the area."

"We'll alert the appropriate people," Fleming said.

O'Brien motioned for Scott, who ended his call with

the general and joined the G-man. They had found the maps of the area, materials used in making the bomb, and a lot of cat food containers in the trash.

But nothing that indicated where the enemy had gone.

THEY RETURNED to Alta Bates. If nothing else, it seemed like the only safe place to be.

O'Brien and Stiletto sat in the crowded lunchroom with cups of quickly cooling coffee in front of them. Stiletto didn't normally drink coffee, but he wasn't in the mood to be fussy about his beverage.

"Casualties are in the triple digits already," O'Brien reported. "There will be more before the day's over. And so many ran from the park when the alarms started that we don't know where they are. Until they start dying, anyway."

"The counter-protest never materialized," Stiletto said.

"Least of our worries, Scott."

"But you don't understand," Stiletto told him and gave him a rundown of the details provided by Sofia McKay.

"This was all part of a propaganda plan?" O'Brien asked.

Stiletto nodded.

"What are you spooks going to do if this guerilla force you describe starts blowing stuff up?"

"I'm not sure," Stiletto said. "We've given everything to you Hoover boys."

The toxicity levels outside prevented anybody from

leaving the hospital. The only good news came from the military weather forecasters, who expected the wind to dissipate the nerve gas cloud within a few more hours. What they couldn't tell was how many would be dead before that happened.

General Ike phoned Stiletto just before midnight.

"A private jet took off from Oakland a half-hour before the explosion," the general said. "We've tracked the plane's identification number to a non-profit group run by Konstantin Hristov, so we finally have evidence of his involvement."

"That's not doing us much good at the moment, sir."

"We've found the plane on radar and are tracking it to see where it lands. Best we can do."

"I'm stuck at the hospital right now, so consider me out of action for the time being."

"I have a feeling," Fleming said, "that you'll be around for the finale, one way or another."

Stiletto told him he wasn't sure it mattered.

CHAPTER EIGHTEEN

STILETTO FLEW home with rage boiling in his belly.

He wanted blood. A lot of it.

There would be no mercy when he finally caught up with the enemy.

As he sat in the CIA plane, having left the situation in Berkeley in the hands of O'Brien and the FBI, he tried to draw in his sketchbook but found his mind too preoccupied. What had he missed? Could there have been something in Monte Carlo that pointed to Moray and Sarto, and he had missed the clue?

Or had the NWRF's operational security been so tight that nothing of value had existed in Monte Carlo?

Killing Zolac wouldn't have been enough. Moray and Sarto were well on their way to carrying out the mission.

Felix Gratien, the accountant, and Sofia McKay, the fake reporter, had only known so much, but would they be any better off had McKay slipped through their grasp?

It wasn't the successful missions Stiletto remembered, but he sure remembered all the failures.

Every now and then one could turn failure into success. Perhaps this time would fall into that category and Stiletto could come home satisfied with the effort.

One way or another, the NWRF was going to pay for what they had done, and according to Stiletto's personal law.

No mercy.

No prisoners.

Only scorched earth.

THE DARK circles under General Fleming's eyes told Stiletto more than he needed to know.

"Nobody's been sleeping," Fleming reported.

"Neither have I," Scott replied. The Agency jet had deposited him at the secure airfield, where he'd hopped into a black sedan and sped to headquarters. He hadn't been out of his clothes in twenty-four hours, and he felt grimy all over. He needed a shower and a rest.

But later.

"Did we track the jet?" Scott asked. He sat in front of the general's desk. A half-glass of water off to Fleming's left showed he'd had his complement of aspirin for the day.

Fleming rotated his PC monitor so Stiletto could view the screen. A couple of key taps displayed a series of pictures in four rows.

"The jet touched down in Germany for fuel," Fleming said, "but we didn't have the crew or passengers detained. Their final destination is what we wanted, and I think we found it."

Fleming clicked on one of the pictures. It filled the screen. A Bombardier Global 8000 jet sat in the center of an airstrip. Open land surrounded the plane, with heavy forest forming a border around the strip.

"Private landing area in the Swiss Alps," he said. "Our satellites recorded two people getting into a Jeep, but we lost them in the mountains. We did, however, find this."

Fleming exited out of the first picture and clicked on another.

A home in the mountains, built on a flat section of land, mountains rising behind it, with a sheer cliff close to the front.

"They were nice enough to leave the Jeep in the drive-way," Fleming said. He zoomed in on the Jeep. It rested near the front of the house, having traveled up a lengthy roadway that trailed through the mountains.

"Who's in the house?"

"Hristov, maybe. Moray and Sarto for sure."

"Give me a full tac team and a couple of gunships, and we'll drop by for tea."

"We may indeed do that," Fleming said. He sat back. "Sofia McKay has been quite willing to talk, by the way. The FBI has managed to round up most of the guerilla teams, and they hadn't even started yet."

"I suppose that's good news."

"Certainly. No more NWRF violence, at least for now. We have our hands full with Berkeley. They're going to be cleaning up there for a long time."

"Final death toll?"

"Let's not dwell on that, Scott. They got us. They got us good. The only thing we can do now is make sure they don't get us again, and breaking the back of the guerilla force was a good start."

"And now we go for the big fish."

"Maybe."

"What?"

"We have to run this up the flagpole. Hristov is not unknown."

"He's a criminal."

"We know that, but we can't prove it. To the rest of the world, he's a reclusive philanthropist."

"He's a mass murderer," Stiletto said. "He thinks he's leading a world revolution. Zolac said so himself. He wants every free man and woman living under a boot at his mercy."

"His Third World food programs have made him a hero in some places," Fleming said.

"What are you telling me, General?"

"We need to be ready for a no—and then we need to be ready for what we're going to do anyway."

"How long?"

"Go home and get some rest," Fleming told him. "I'll call you."

Stiletto rose from his chair. "Sometimes this job sucks. Sir."

He started for the door.

"It's the spy business, Scott," Fleming said.

Stiletto didn't stop to respond. Setbacks, delays, and downright interference from the top was always justified by "it's the spy business" but that wasn't enough for Scott.

The enemy was out there. They knew his name. There had to be something more they could do.

STILETTO ENTERED his empty apartment and fell onto the couch.

He pulled out his phone and selected his daughter's phone number from his contact list. She wasn't living in Berkeley or anywhere near California, but he felt the need to try to reach her. Of course, she didn't answer. Stiletto hesitated to leave a message, but when the recorded greeting stopped, he couldn't bring himself to simply hang up.

"Felicia, it's your father," he said. "I'm sure you're watching the news. Don't be frightened. We're working on it. I love you."

He hung up.

And felt like an idiot. He was telling her not to be frightened when he knew very well that there was plenty to be frightened about.

He'd also told her too much, not that it mattered.

He purposely left the television off so as not to be exposed to what the media was saying. They wouldn't be saying anything productive anyway, and the talking heads, as usual, contributed nothing but wrong information and barely informed opinions.

It was all a big joke, a giant freak show for ratings.

Stiletto held the phone on his lap with his jaw set tight. The mission had gone from prevention, to revenge.

And Stiletto would show no the enemy no mercy.

THE PHONE rang.

Stiletto jerked awake and answered without looking at the caller ID. There was no need.

"Yes, sir?"

"A direct assault has been denied," Fleming said.

"Why?"

"The reasons we talked about, Scott. No need to repeat them. The President and the Director have agreed that we cannot go public and identify Hristov as the perpetrator. We're cooking up a cover story."

"It won't hold."

"Not your problem."

Stiletto gripped the phone tightly. "What *is* my problem, General? Or do I keep sitting on my ass?"

"The United States will not officially issue a termination protocol against Hristov. We are going to need a proxy."

"Okay."

"Any ideas?"

Stiletto stood up and paced the room. His mind raced, and a name popped into his head.

"Devlin Marcus," he said.

"The mercenary colonel?"

"He helped put us on Zolac's trail at the beginning of this mess. He might want to be included in the resolution."

"Do you think he'd do it if the price was right?"

"For him, the price is everything."

"Where do we find him?"

"Leave that to me, sir. I only need a flight to Italy and time to reach him."

Fleming said he'd better get started.

STILETTO LANDED in Milan with a renewed sense of optimism and a blank check from the United States government in his pocket.

Sort of.

A briefcase full of unmarked American dollars certainly sufficed.

Two million dollars, precisely.

Stiletto hoped it would be enough. He rented a car at the airport and drove to Marcus's home. There was no sense in trying the casino. If Marcus wasn't there, he'd eventually return to the house on the lake.

Stiletto drove up to the gate and announced himself to the guard posted in a small wooden shack. The guard that hadn't been in place the first time he'd visited.

"Tell Marcus his American friend Scott is here with a business proposal."

The guard nodded and picked up a phone. He spoke, listened for a moment, and told Stiletto, "Boss says to go in."

Stiletto nodded and waited for the guard to open the

gate. It swung open slowly, without a squeak, on well-oiled hinges.

Stiletto traveled up the circular driveway. The property looked nice in the daylight. Green grass, and a statue with a water feature in the center of the drive.

Devlin Marcus, dressed casually, waited at the front steps. Stiletto exited the car with briefcase in hand.

"Must be some important business," the mercenary leader remarked.

"I'll take a drink if you have one," Scott said.

"Follow me to my office."

Marcus poured scotch over two ice cubes and handed the glass to Scott. He sat in front of the man's desk once again as Marcus eased into his chair.

"So?"

"I need a wrecking crew," Stiletto said. He outlined the mission and the reasons the CIA refused to carry out the job.

Marcus sipped from his glass and regarded Stiletto over the rim for a moment.

"I have the men," he assured Scott, "and the gunships. What I need is money."

"I have two million in the briefcase. Cash."

"I could ask for more." Marcus brushed back the hair over his right ear.

"I could get you more."

"I've been watching what happened in California," Marcus said. "It's terrible. Those responsible shouldn't be allowed to breathe clean air."

"Does that mean you'll help?"

"The money will be sufficient."

Stiletto put his glass on the desk, picked up the briefcase, and handed it to Marcus. "Count it."

Marcus snapped the locks and lifted the lid. "Won't be necessary. I know you're good for it."

"When can we start?"

"I'll call my two team leaders, and we'll get started right away."

Marcus picked up the phone on the desk.

KONSTANTIN HRISTOV resembled a toad.

Short and fat, with a face that looked like it had been rubbed against concrete and then decorated with age spots, wrinkles, and a mole or two, the European crime boss / philanthropist known as the Bulgarian stood alone in a conference room facing a wall of television monitors. On the table in front of him sat a panel with which he could control the monitors and the volume of the men speaking. He stood with his spotted and overly fleshy hands behind his back.

His suit fit his heavy body well, as it should have since all of his clothes were custom-fitted to his frame. Only from the neck up did he look like the near wreck that he was, although somehow his system kept humming along as he approached his nineties.

Faces on the monitors looked back at him—the faces

of the leaders of the New World Revolutionary Front. Had the operation in Berkeley gone as planned, Heinrich Zolac would have once again met with the men in the high rise where he'd first announced their plans, but with Zolac dead, the responsibility fell to Hristov. It was one of the few times the other leaders had seen him, but they all knew who he was, and, worse, the violence he was so capable of.

"Zolac is dead," Hristov announced. He didn't expect the men to react strongly, and none did. A few blinked their eyes. One looked surprised.

"What happened?" asked a man in a corner monitor. Hristov knew him as Arnold Bell, one of Zolac's trusted confidants.

"While our nerve gas attack in the United States was successful, the Americans caught up with our people at the last moment. Zolac did not survive. Moray and Sarto, however, managed to escape, and have joined me here in the Alps."

Bell continued, "Zolac went there to—"

"No longer the point, Mr. Bell. With the loss of McKay and Gratien, knowing how close the Americans came to stopping us in California and how our second-phase guerilla attacks have been thwarted, we must now consider ourselves fully exposed."

Another man, Grunberg, his face and bald head in a lower monitor, said: "What does that mean?"

"We must go into hiding. They will be looking for us."

Silence answered the statement.

"There was always the danger of this happening," Hristov said, "and I am sure we have all planned for a rainy day, have we not?"

Grunts and nods in reply.

"So please take measures to make sure you are not caught in the net," Hristov requested. He paused, straightened a little, and continued, "Now, better news. Despite our troubles, the nerve gas attack was a complete success. Today we are reading of a death toll that has stabilized in the low thousands."

"If the attack did not lead to the disruption we had hoped to create," Arnold Bell asked, "how can the mission be considered a success?"

"Revolution takes time," Hristov replied calmly. "We still have our allies in the media and the politicians in our pockets who will push our agenda, albeit in a way that's more palatable to the American public. They will work to change minds, and we will work to bring about our vision. There are elements that McKay did not know about, and what she doesn't know, she cannot tell.

"While we are in hiding," Hristov continued, "we will develop new plans. I have several already in mind. We will learn from the missteps we made in California, and the next operation will provide us with the results we seek."

Hristov stopped talking. The faces on the monitors stared back at him, the men waiting for more. Better, they weren't objecting. Nobody was too upset about the problems encountered with the US.

Which meant they were still loyal to the cause.

"This will be our last communication until further notice," Hristov said. "When we speak again, you will be notified by contacts familiar to you, so there will be no doubt it is I who wish to address you once more. Are there any questions?"

There were none.

"Farewell for now, and good luck."

Hristov touched a button on the panel before him and the monitors went blank.

A door opened behind him.

"Sir."

Hristov turned.

Robert Moray, a rifle slung across his back, stood in the doorway. Hristov had considered killing him and the Sarto woman upon their return, but realized they had their uses, so he ordered them to join the guards.

"What is it?"

"Attack force approaching."

"How many?"

"Three helicopter gunships, unknown number of troops."

Hristov didn't hesitate.

"Shoot them down."

Moray nodded and departed.

CHAPTER NINETEEN

STILETTO LOOKED at the twenty faces watching him and hoped he wasn't leading the men to their deaths.

Marcus had introduced his two team leaders only as Hardball and Short Fuse. Hardball, a tall, barrel-chested white man, derived his nickname because his bald head looked like the tip of a full metal jacketed bullet. Short Fuse, a short and stocky black fellow, was the resident explosives expert, and often rigged his charges with a short fuse, hence his moniker. Stiletto wasn't surprised they kept their real names a secret. Most mercenaries did.

The rest of the twenty, he didn't know yet. He leaned against a table at the front of the room, watching Devlin Marcus give the general briefing.

Showing the satellite imagery Stiletto had brought on a thumb drive on a large flat-screen mounted on the wall behind him, Marcus talked about the terrain, and especially Hristov's estate. The multiple buildings, all connected, sat on a flat section with a mountain rising in the back. They identified an area not twenty yards from the buildings where three helicopters sat. A winding road led through the mountains to the area in front of the estate, and the pictures showed armed troopers milling about.

Marcus gave them the bad news. They had no idea how much resistance they would face. They had no idea if the target, Hristov, had any secret escape routes. They had no idea of the security: if there were any mines or trip-wires rigged on the approach.

The mercenaries didn't seem to care. It was another day at the office for them. Each man understood the final instructions, though. Go in and kill everybody. No prisoners. Collect any and all intelligence information, but leaving nobody alive was the primary goal.

The crew exited to pack and check equipment. Marcus said they'd depart in an hour.

Stiletto couldn't shake the feeling that this was a suicide mission.

STILETTO FELT right at home in the Huey helicopter gunship.

He rode in the lead helicopter's cabin with Short Fuse, Hardball, and three other mercs. The rest of the space contained extra gear for the mission, while the remaining mercenaries flew in the other two choppers behind theirs. The helicopters were outfitted with the usual Huey gunship armaments, including a side-mounted M-60 machine gun. A pair of rocket pods extended from either side, along with twin rotating M134 mini-guns. The choppers would provide needed air support once the main force struck the estate.

Marcus rode up front in the co-pilot's seat and radioed back that they were getting close to the landing zone. Stiletto and the rest of the crew acknowledged over their communication headsets and began prepping for the exit. The doors on either side of the fuselage were shut, but that did not block out the loud hammering of the rotor blades above the cabin.

Stiletto, seated nearest the left door, looked out the window at one of the other choppers. They would be pre-paring to touch down as well, and the mission would be in full go mode. Nothing to stop them now. No last-minute abort-abort orders from up top that were so common in these missions.

When the first chopper exploded, Stiletto didn't quite believe what he saw. The fireball was obvious enough, the spread of debris and bodies undeniable as gravity took over, but then Devlin Marcus was shouting about incoming missiles. The pilot executed a sweeping evasive maneuver that crushed Stiletto and the other mercenaries together, straining them against the seat straps, the turbine engines whining.

The chopper shuddered violently.

"We've been hit by debris!" Marcus shouted over the radio. "Other two choppers destroyed, and we're going down!"

Smoke drifted into the cabin. When the chopper straightened out, Stiletto lunged for the door release bar and pulled up, and the door slid open. Fresh air rushed in, blowing out the smoke, and also showing the ground spinning below them as the chopper circled to find a flat landing space.

Nothing but rocky ground below.

"Going in hot!" Marcus shouted. Everybody grabbed for any available handhold as the ground rushed toward them at an accelerated rate.

The landing skids hit hard.

"OUT OUT out!"

Stiletto pulled the seat straps free and fell sideways out of the chopper, which sat at an odd angle against a hill, having skidded along the slope until mercifully stopping against a cluster of boulders. Smoke choked the cabin, the underside of the bird ripped by flying chunks from the other two choppers.

Short Fuse piled out, followed by Hardball and the other three mercenaries, and they began unloading the spare equipment. The pilot's door was jammed by a boulder, so Marcus, on the opposite side, exited first, then turned to help the pilot get free. Soon the pilot had a rifle and fighting gear in hand.

Marcus checked everybody for injuries. There were cuts, bruises, and assorted contusions, but nobody was bleeding. They rallied near a tall tree, grateful for its shade. Stiletto and another merc took up security positions, scanning the terrain around them. There were some dry parts among grassy parts, the terrain rolling up and down and flat in sections. The ominous jagged peaks surrounding them were a majestic sight, but now was not the time to revel in God's glory. The enemy would be coming to finish off survivors.

Marcus performed a headcount. "Seven," he said, cursing and looking back for any signs of the other two choppers. Smoke crawled skyward in the distance.

"They're gone, Dev," Stiletto told him.

Marcus cursed again. "They'll pay for this."

"If we don't start moving, we'll be sitting ducks," Stiletto said.

Marcus pulled out a map and spread the paper on the ground. He noted their current position and the location of Hristov's estate. "Gonna be a long march," he said. "Squad, on me. Combat formation. Be ready for anything."

Stiletto and the mercenaries moved out in a V formation. He wondered what was coming next. If the enemy already knew they were here, how much harder would it be to reach the target?

There was nothing to do but put one foot in front of the other, so that was what Stiletto did. The next challenge would arrive soon enough.

MORAY, LEANING out the side of his own helicopter, hands on the twin-handles of the door-mounted machine gun, fired a burst into the wreckage of one of the downed choppers. There were a few scattered bodies, most of which didn't move, but one or two of which looked like they were trying to crawl. Moray fixed that with a couple of strafing runs.

In the cabin behind him were four Hristov soldiers ready for action. And Kylie. She watched over Moray's shoulder. If they found any survivors on the run, the chopper would land, and the troops would engage and hopefully solve the problem. As for the bodies and the wreckage, neither Moray nor Hristov saw any cause for concern. They were out in the middle of nowhere. Plenty of time to get rid of the corpses and make it look like nothing had ever happened.

They flew over the other downed chopper, but this time Moray saved his ammunition. It was quite plain that no one remained alive on the ground.

Over to the third.

It was harder to find, having traveled farther than the other two, but when Moray saw the machine resting on the slope of a hill, stopped only by a well-placed boulder, he tensed because there were no bodies about.

"Set us down," Moray said into his radio.

"No flat areas, sir," the pilot reported back.

"We'll have to rappel," Moray said, signaling the other troops, who began hooking lines into their combat harnesses. The pilot held the chopper steady as Moray, Kylie, and the four troopers descended to the ground, Moray waving to the pilot when the last of them touched down. The chopper pulled up and veered off, staying in close orbit as Moray ordered the men to take up security positions while he and Kylie investigated the downed chopper.

"How many aboard?" Kylie said.

"Look at the footprints," Moray said. "There's a bunch, but they all run together at this point and head over there."

They ran to the tree, the disturbed dirt and footprints telling a story, but a cloudy one. It wasn't until they found the marching tracks, where the attack force had spread into a V formation, that they obtained a decent count of what they faced.

"Six," Moray said, "maybe seven, give or take one or two."

"Call back the chopper?"

"No, they can't be far. If they saw the chopper, they've taken cover. We can keep them pinned as long as the chopper is in the air and pick 'em off." Moray whistled to the other four troopers, who quickly rallied, and Moray explained his plan.

Moray updated the pilot before moving out. The chopper continued in wide circles, the whipping rotors blades riding the gentle wind as it blew through the area.

He led his team forward.

STILETTO, MARCUS, and the mercenary team hustled down a slope and across a rocky gorge. A stream lay ahead, not very wide or deep, and they splashed through. The cluster of trees in front of them seemed a million miles away, but they would otherwise be caught in the open by the approaching helicopter, and there was nowhere else to hide

They finally gained the shelter of the trees and took positions that kept them relatively out of sight. Marcus scooted next to Stiletto, who lay near the edge of the tree line, the chopper in plain view as it circled.

"Cleanup crew," Marcus stated. "They saw our tracks."

"I didn't see the chopper land, so that's their air support," Stiletto replied. "Lots of guns on either side."

"We could sure use that machine."

"Right now, I'm more concerned with the troops they dropped off."

Short Fuse laid down beside Marcus.

"How're our rear flanks, Short?" Marcus asked.

"Slope," the bomb expert said. "It gets pretty steep. This is a lousy place for a battle."

"Well, here it comes," Stiletto said, hefting his weapon as figures appeared over the top of the rise they'd just cleared.

"Get ready!" Marcus yelled.

Stiletto tucked the stock of the Heckler & Koch HK416 into his shoulder. The automatic rifle, with its compact ten-inch barrel and open sights had a familiar feel, since it resembled the M-4 and M-16 rifle families of the US military with which Stiletto was so familiar. The 5.56mm chambering was also well known to him, and the rifle felt like a natural extension of his body as he lined up the front and rear sights on the approaching targets.

"Let 'em have it!" Marcus called.

Stiletto squeezed the trigger.

CHAPTER TWENTY

THE FIRST two rounds left Stiletto's weapon, an enemy trooper at the top of the rise falling as the 5.56mm rounds ripped into his midsection. The fighters behind him dropped for cover, shooting over the rise, bullets nipping at the trees and sending bits of bark and twigs flying in all directions. Stiletto adjusted his aim and fired another burst. More gunfire from the other mercs' HK416 rifles crackled around him.

The Alps were for skiing, not for fighting, Stiletto thought, adjusting his aim again.

The whipping rotor blades of the helicopter grew louder as the flying machine approached, coming in low, and even Stiletto didn't need to be told what was coming next. He shouted, "Incoming!" as smoke puffed from the left-mounted missile pod. The 12.7mm rockets whooshed toward the trees, trailing a short tail of flame.

Stiletto left the tree and ran, other mercs and Hard-ball running with him. When the rockets hit, the ground shook, and the trio of explosions rattled Stiletto's bones. The shockwave knocked him off his feet, and he went flying past another tree trunk to land hard on the ground on the other side. Heavy machine gun fire punctuated the rocket blasts, sections of trees falling and several screams piercing the cacophony. Stiletto rolled onto his back. The rocket impacts had started a blaze at the front of the tree line.

He dropped flat and opened fire on the enemy troops running through the flames to penetrate the trees and assault the mercenaries hidden within. The HK416 rocked in both hands. A trooper fell back, his gun firing skyward in reflex as another pivoted to line up on Scott. A blast from off to Stiletto's left impacted with the man's face, and he left behind a bloody mist as he joined his fallen comrade.

Stiletto pulled back to go left to join whichever of Marcus' mercenaries was firing from that side, took two steps and—

Scott's head snapped back as the toe of a boot connected with his chin. He fell back, rolling and bumping into a tree, his vision spinning as he tried to get back to his feet. Another boot slammed into his stomach, and air left him. The boot swept toward him again, and Stiletto grabbed the foot in both hands and twisted. A woman yelled, but the scream choked off when she hit the ground. Stiletto jumped to his feet.

The woman, who had short red hair, didn't stay on the ground long. She came at him with a flurry of spinning kicks and short punches that Stiletto could only deflect as he recovered from her first strike. He dodged to one side as her long left leg swept up and out, missing his head by half an inch. As she followed through with her spin, he struck. A solid kick to her midsection sent the woman sprawling, and Stiletto clawed for the .45 in his hip holster. He drew the gun but she was on him again, knocking the pistol from his hand and landing a trio of blows in the center of his chest.

Breath left Stiletto as he fell hard on his back, the sounds of the battle still raging around him. The whipping rotor blades of the helicopter, the hammering of machine-gun fire, voices yelling throughout the hell of battle. Stiletto tried to move, but his limbs didn't respond.

The woman's face looked down on him. She was blurry. Another face, male, joined hers, and the man said, "We have a prize for Hristov."

Then his vision faded and Stiletto heard nothing more.

MARCUS BLASTED another enemy soldier in the chest, the man falling back. Nearby, Short Fuse worked the trigger of his sidearm and downed another.

There were dead men all around. Most were his men; the rest, the enemy. The rockets and cannon fire from the chopper had decimated his squad.

"Fall back!" Marcus shouted. He and Short Fuse, joined by Hardball, fled the tree line and headed back across the gorge to the hillside. The flames from the rockets ate more and more at the cluster of trees, thick smoke drifting with the wind. The chopper was somewhere on the other side of the tree cluster, still low to the ground. When Marcus, Short Fuse, and Hardball reached the hill, they ran along the side until they were far enough away to see the back of the clump. And the chopper. A man had somebody over his shoulder, another figure watching for threats with a rifle. Marcus knew the man being carried was Stiletto.

With the rest of his team dead and Stiletto now in enemy hands, Marcus felt his heart sink. Stiletto was a good man. All of his men were good men and good fighters. They deserved more than being slaughtered at the hands of an enemy who planned more of the same against people who couldn't defend themselves.

"What do we do, boss?" Hardball asked. His face was covered in sweat and grime, and his combat fatigues were torn in spots.

The helicopter drifted skyward, the nose dipping as it headed for home base.

"We go back," Marcus said. "We gather as much gear and ammo as we can and we carry on. We aren't leaving here until we're either dead or the enemy is."

"Sounds good to me," Short Fuse said.

"Hardball?"

"We don't have much of a chance, boss."

"We've been paid to do a job, and we're going to do it."

"How do we get up the mountain?"

Marcus had to admit he had no answer.

"We can't leave the job unfinished," he said instead. "One way or another, we complete our task, or we die. Okay?"

Hardball nodded. "Lead the way, boss."

"Come on, then," Marcus said.

He started back for the trees.

THE UNCONSCIOUS American lay on the floor of the cabin, his hands zip-tied behind his back. Moray and Kylie rode securely in the cabin seats.

Moray stared at the man, his face unknown to him, wondering if he was the same fellow who had caused so much trouble for them during the recovery of the ZH4 in Iraq. There was another concern on his mind—the fact that the attack force had known where to find them. There was only one answer, and Moray knew it made him and Kylie a liability in Hristov's eyes.

The only way the attack force had reached them was because they had tracked the plane out of Oakland. How long had it taken to find the address he gave at the rental car company? The house itself, and Zolac's body? Or had the Americans discovered clues overseas in Monte Carlo and Austria, as Zolac had originally feared?

Either way, if Hristov wasn't happy with the prisoner and what he might be able to extract from the man's mind, Moray imagined that there was a target on his back. And Kylie's.

He'd have to figure out what to do about that.

He glanced at Kylie, but her attention was focused on the sharp peaks of the Alps and their snowy caps.

Presently the chopper touched down in front of the main building. A smattering of armed troops milled about, their weapons at the ready. The chief of the guard force approached Moray as he and Kylie unloaded Stiletto.

"Any left?"

"A few escaped. Not many."

"Best guess?"

"Two or three."

The guard chief nodded. They wouldn't need to spare another patrol to go out and finish the job. A force of that size, if it could be called such a thing, wouldn't last long in a frontal assault if they were desperate enough to attempt one. Extraction was their best bet. Moray figured they had a rendezvous point somewhere that was their only concern now that they'd been wiped out.

Kylie and Moray carried Stiletto's unconscious body between them and entered the building. The estate didn't have any holding cells since it wasn't meant to house prisoners even temporarily. They decided to put him in the basement gym used by the guard force. There, they set him on the floor while Moray helped Kylie take down a heavy punching bag that was hooked to a rope and pulley system, by which the heavy bag could be raised and lowered. They undid the zip-tie behind Stiletto's back and zipped his wrists together in front so they could raise his hands over his head, and lowered the hook far enough to connect it to the zip tie. Moray and Kylie huffed and puffed while they pulled on the rope to raise Stiletto off the floor. The American's body swayed back and forth a little, his head hanging low.

Moray and Kylie turned to leave the gym and stopped at the sight of Konstantin Hristov in the doorway.

"I did not ask for prisoners," the Bulgarian said.

Moray explained who the man was and that he might have information valuable to them.

Hristov frowned.

"Stay with him until he wakes up," Hristov said. "Then I will confront him."

Hristov turned and departed.

Moray and Kylie exchanged nervous glances.

She knew as well as Moray did that they were on thin ice.

HRISTOV SHOULD never have let Moray and the woman reach the estate.

It would have been easy to neutralize them during their stopover in Berlin.

The Americans had tracked the jet, no mistake.

Well. There was nothing to do about that now, other than follow through with what he'd told the others in the video conference.

It was time to go into hiding until further notice. His next operation, he decided, had to be much bigger than Berkeley; something that took the United States so solidly out of play that the nation would never recover. Once the US fell, the rest of the world would topple. Victory for the revolution.

Perhaps a nuclear attack.

Perhaps several at once.

Hristov returned to his office on the top floor of the main building and poured himself a drink, then sat behind his desk. The forward wall had been replaced by windows, and he looked out on the Alps in the distance and the valley stretching to infinity below. It was a peaceful view, and one he would miss.

He missed it already as he sipped his drink.

Moray and Sarto still needed to pay for the trouble they'd caused. Their haste in escaping California was something he could not forgive.

He'd explain it to them later.

Before he had them killed.

STILETTO AWOKE with a start and groaned. His whole body hurt and felt like it was being pulled apart. When he looked up at how the zip-tie was hooked to the pulley and then down at his feet and the space between them and the floor, he understood why. Gravity sucked.

He let his body dangle and caught his breath, tilting his head back to look up at the ceiling, if for nothing more than to give his neck relief from hanging forward for so long.

"You're awake."

Stiletto moved his head to see the redheaded woman standing before him. She'd been in a chair beside the door.

"This is a strange torture chamber," Scott said.

"Some people would look at it that way, I guess."

"Then they're wasting their membership money."

The woman actually laughed.

"Where's the rest of my team?"

A half-smile this time. She spoke into a handheld radio, but Stiletto paid no attention as he tipped his head back again. He wasn't looking at the ceiling this time, but at the hook he was hanging from. If he could get his hands on the chain above the hook, he might conceivably be able to lift the zip-tie off the hook and drop free.

Gravity was his worst enemy at this point.

He looked down at the woman. She lowered his radio and regarded him with curiosity.

"You were in Iraq?" he asked.

She nodded.

"Too bad about Porter," he said.

"You knew him?"

"We identified him later," Stiletto told her. "I like to know the people I kill for my scrapbook. By the way, what's your name?"

"You won't live long enough to find out."

The door behind her opened and a wiry man entered, holding the door for an older man. Konstantin Hristov. He looked worse in person than in pictures. Pictures didn't quite capture the fleshy-toad resemblance.

The old man stood before Stiletto and blinked a few times.

"Hello, Hristov," Stiletto said.

"I am frankly surprised," the Bulgarian said, "that you Americans would bother to come to kill me."

"We do all kinds of things when we're mad," Stiletto stated.

"And you're mad at me?"

"If you don't know why, I'm not going to tell you."

Hristov laughed. "Are you the only American in this attack? Who else are we facing?"

Stiletto held back a grin. Who else? That meant some of the others survived.

"You're facing the best of the best," Stiletto said.

"Considering most of them are dead, they couldn't have been that good."

"You'll find out the hard way, old-timer."

"Insults are the last vestige of the desperate, my friend, and you have certainly come to your end. Kylie here is a martial arts expert, as you discovered. Since you are hanging from the ceiling like the punching bag you replaced, I think she should take advantage and use you for her daily practice session. Wouldn't that be nice, my dear?"

"It would be lovely," Kylie said.

"We will leave you two alone, then," Hristov said. "Come and find us in my office when you're done, my dear."

Hristov departed and the other man followed, closing

the door behind them.

Kylie Sarto looked Stiletto up and down.

"This might hurt a bit."

"Do your worst, you silly bitch."

Her first blow landed dead-center in his belly.

CHAPTER TWENTY-ONE

PUNCH. PUNCH.

Kick. Spin-kick. Punch.

The blows landed with the weight of bricks, but all Stiletto could do was hang there and take the punishment. He kept his legs together to protect his groin, but she didn't see him begin to bend his legs at the knees and raise them slightly.

Punch. Kick.

Breath left Scott, his eyes shut tight. His grunts and groans escaped despite his best efforts, and each one seemed to light up the woman's eyes.

Punch. Punch.

His midsection felt like it was on fire. She couldn't reach his upper body without standing on the chair, and she hadn't decided to do that yet.

Spin-kick.

The kick landed on Stiletto's side, and he lost all ability to keep his muscles tense. His legs dropped limp, and he felt his body sinking despite being hung from a hook. The blows were taking a toll, and if Stiletto didn't counter-attack soon, he'd be out of the fight permanently.

Breathless, she stopped for a moment. Removing her fatigue blouse, she tossed it on the chair and limbered up some more in her green tank top and camouflage pants. A K-Bar fighting knife rode on the left of her pistol belt, and a Beretta 92FS was holstered on the right. She removed both items and placed those on the chair as well.

She bounced on the balls of her feet for a moment, grinning at him.

"Ready for the next round?"

Stiletto spat at her. He missed, but the point was made. A red flush crawled up her neck.

She launched a high kick at his chin.

DEVLIN MARCUS, Hardball, and Short Fuse watched through the brush as three Hristov troopers serviced the chopper used to attack them. Two more fully-loaded helicopters sat on the pad as well.

Just like the satellite pictures had shown.

Marcus scanned the area carefully. To make a mistake now would sign Stiletto's death warrant. He nodded at Short Fuse and Hardball and hefted the HK416 to his shoulder.

There were only the three guards, and they only carried sidearms. No rifles present.

Marcus fired once and one of the troopers fell forward, landing inside the chopper. Parts of his skull decorated the cabin. Short Fuse and Hardball opened fire on the other two, their short bursts echoing through the valley.

Marcus broke cover and ran for the chopper off to the left. They needed a fully-loaded machine for the strike. Marcus climbed behind the controls while Short Fuse and Hardball jumped into the cabin. Hardball racked the action on the door-mounted machine gun, a Browning .50-caliber, and locked a belt of ammo into the receiver.

The rotors started slowly and gained speed, the motor whining. The speed increased, the brush around the landing pad blowing as if a hurricane had struck, and Marcus raised the helicopter off the ground. He gained altitude, spinning the nose around a hundred and eighty degrees and dipping forward to speed toward the Hristov estate.

Marcus worked the cyclic and collective to move the chopper up and down as the geography dictated. He zeroed in on the mountain peak atop which Hristov's hideaway lay.

When they were close enough, Marcus spun the chopper so Hardball's side faced the building. "Let 'em have it!"

Hardball pulled the trigger, and the weapon shuddered as the heavy caliber bullets flashed from the muzzle. Troops on the ground dropped, and Hardball peppered the building with a long string of slugs.

Marcus spun the chopper around and fired rockets into the building. The rockets ran dry as explosions lit the hillside, secondary blasts launching debris in all directions. Hardball hosed anything that moved below with the big .50 until the weapon ran dry.

"We're out of ammo!" he called.

Marcus put the chopper down, and he, Hardball, and Short Fuse hustled out.

As they ran into the building, no guards challenged them.

KYLIE SARTO started on Stiletto's backside. Stiletto hung like a piece of meat. There was nothing he could do with her back there.

He let his head fall forward. It wasn't hard. The blows were draining whatever strength he tried to keep, but he was still short of unconsciousness. Most of his body felt numb after so many hits.

She stopped.

Her laugh was like a chime as she came around in front again.

"I think," she said, breathing heavily, "I'm actually too tired to continue."

Stiletto put his knees together.

"How about that?" she said.

"How about that indeed," he told her. With a yell to muster everything he had, he brought his bent legs up perpendicular to the floor, launched his feet forward, and slammed the heels into Kylie's upper chest. With a yelp she flew backward, the back of her knees colliding with the chair. Her lower body stopped its backward momentum but her upper body carried on, her head arching back to smack into the wall.

Her skull cracked like a peanut shell, and the audible snap echoed through the room. She collapsed on the tiled floor, her wide eyes staring at the ceiling.

Stiletto let out another cry as he strained his body. He put one hand above the hook, then the other, and his shoulders and back burned as he pulled upward. He thought the effort would tear him apart, but then the zip-tie jumped off the hook. When he let go, his body crumpled to the floor and he lay there gasping.

Then the explosions began.

The building shook. Machine guns opened up, their hammering consistent, the unmistakable sounds of a .50-caliber music to Scott's ears. It had to be Marcus and his crew, or whoever was left. But the cavalry had arrived, and it was time to bring this mission to a close.

Stiletto rolled to his side, then painfully gained his feet. He staggered over to the chair. He grabbed the Beretta 92FS and checked the load, finding a spare magazine on dead Kylie's belt. He dropped the magazine into a side pocket, gripping the Beretta tightly in his right hand as he left the room and advanced down the hall.

The house continued shaking with multiple explosions. Stiletto moved fast. Ceiling plaster rained down as he neared the end of the hall and its stairway, taking the steps two at a time to the first floor. Wide-open room, furniture, and fancy decorations. He stopped short as three gunmen entered the room, and lowered the pistol as he recognized Marcus, Short Fuse, and Hardball.

"You're late!" Stiletto called.

"No store in this town has any Guinness," Marcus explained.

MORAY AND HRISTOV, in the top floor office, hugged the ground.

"They'll come up the stairs," Moray said. He held an automatic rifle close to his side.

"This is all your fault!" Hristov shouted.

"No time for that now," Moray told him.

"Oh, there's time," Hristov said. He breathlessly rose to his hands and knees. Air rushed in from the sections of the wall-length window shattered by the chopper attack. Not all of the glass had broken. He crawled to his desk, opening a drawer. He removed a Walther P-38, the grips of the nine-millimeter pistol warming in his hands.

Moray didn't notice. His eyes were fixed on the top of the stairs that led into the office.

"Moray!"

He turned.

Hristov leveled the Walther. "All your fault!"

"No!"

Hristov fired twice, then twice more. The bullets punched into Moray's body and pinned him to the carpet.

Hristov moved awkwardly to Moray's body, turning him over. He picked up the rifle, examined it for a minute, and threw it down in disgust. He didn't know how to operate the weapon, but he did know how to use the grenades on Moray's combat harness. He pulled one free. Jamming the Walther in the waistband of his trousers, he pulled the pin and turned to face the stairs.

STILETTO LED Marcus, Hardball, and Short Fuse into the next room and the steps leading upstairs. The shooting and yelling above couldn't be ignored.

"Hristov!" Stiletto shouted. "Make it easy and kill yourself! Otherwise, I will tear you apart!"

The first grenade dropped down the steps, *thump-thump*. Stiletto and the others scattered for cover, the furniture providing ample places to hide. The explosion rocked the room and debris flew in all directions. Another grenade *thump-thumped* down the steps, falling into the crater in the floor created by the first blast. The second explosion shattered what remained of the windows and sparked a fire.

Stiletto, hunkered behind a couch, waited. His ears were ringing from the blasts, the pain running through his body like a river a distant memory now as his mind raced with the possibility of finally destroying his quarry.

Hristov had nothing left to drop.

Stiletto looked around to see the other three rising from their hiding spaces. Stiletto announced, "I'm going up. Cover me."

Marcus nodded.

Stiletto started up the steps, the Beretta extended in

both hands. At the top of the steps, he paused. That toad Hristov lay directly ahead, and he had a gun in his right fist.

"Put it down," the Bulgarian said. "You can't win. I have you covered."

Hristov's hand was shaking, the P-38's muzzle shifting left and right with the movement.

"Disgusting old man," Stiletto growled. "Can't hold a gun straight."

Hristov's finger tightened on the Walther's trigger, and Stiletto dropped. The nine-millimeter stingers exploded overhead, then the automatic locked open, empty. Hristov groaned.

Stiletto cleared the steps and stood above Hristov with the Beretta aimed at the man's head.

"Do you pray?"

Hristov cursed.

"I didn't think so."

He waited.

"Kill me," Hristov demanded.

"Look at me."

"No."

Stiletto shot Hristov through the right hand. The old man screamed, pulling the destroyed hand close to his body. His eyes snapped to Stiletto's, a reaction he couldn't control.

"That wasn't so hard," Scott said.

Stiletto fired again, and the old man's head split

like a watermelon. Bits of the man's skull landed on Stiletto's boots.

No big deal. He could clean the boots later.

CHAPTER TWENTY-TWO

CARLTON WEBB, the Director of Central Intelligence, faced the President across his desk in the Oval Office.

The President sat with his hands folded on his lap, his face thoughtful as he listened to Webb's briefing. There were no papers to review and no photos to share. The conversation technically wasn't happening. Webb was officially somewhere else and had not signed the White House log.

When he finished, the President said nothing for a moment. Finally, he took a deep breath.

"I'm glad to hear the mission was successful," he said. "I'm sorry for the loss of life. On our side, of course."

"Our man brought back a pile of information as well, sir," Webb said. "We have names, locations, and other pertinent information about the New World Revolutionary Front that we didn't have before. We can now systematically dismantle the organization and capture or do away with everybody within."

"But what about the Vice President? The members of Congress that you now know were working with them?"

"I've been giving that some thought," Webb said. "I propose that we confront these individuals with what we know and suggest that they resign to spend more time with their families."

"And what happens with the information?"

Webb smiled. "We keep it safe. You never know when we might need it for something."

"I think that's a fine plan," the President agreed.

"I THINK you've earned a rest," General Ike told his agent.

"Having just spent two days in the hospital, sir," Stiletto said, "I think I've had enough."

"You have broken ribs, a concussion, and various bruises and abrasions. How you're even sitting here surprises me."

"I walked it off."

"Go home. I'll see you in two weeks."

Stiletto didn't move.

"Something else on your mind?"

"We're not done. The information I brought back—"

"Stop. The information you brought back is not only still being processed but will be acted upon by people other than you. Your role in this operation is over, Scott. You are not the only agent who works on my staff."

Stiletto still didn't move.

"What else?"

"This was a tough one, sir."

"They'll get tougher," Fleming said. "They always do. The thing is, so do we, and you won't notice the next one because this one prepared you for it."

"I can't help thinking we missed something along the way."

"Maybe we did. When you're in my position, you'll have to deal with even more questions. You don't think I sit here wondering what else we could have done? If we hadn't missed that somebody would try and hijack the ZH4 in the beginning, we might have avoided all of this."

Stiletto nodded.

"We do our best," Fleming told him, "and the rest is up to God."

"A bit double-edged there, sir."

"True, but we aren't supermen. Sometimes we have to rely on something more powerful. Despite the losses, I'd say we made out okay. In fact, I'd say Devlin Marcus is going to be a valuable asset in the days and months ahead."

Stiletto nodded again.

"Now go. See you in two weeks."

Stiletto put both hands on the arm of his chair and pushed to his feet. He winced a little.

"You walked it off, huh?" the general inquired.

"Well, you know," Stiletto replied as he started for the door, "getting old sucks. Takes longer to bounce back."

"Take it easy."

"Yes, sir, General."

STILETTO DROVE home in his Trans Am. As soon as he staggered into his bedroom, he fell onto the mattress. He laughed a little. He was ending the mission on the mattress, same as he'd begun.

He'd take the two weeks to recover, try and find something to do to keep his mind off the things he didn't want to think about, and when it was time to go back to work, he'd perform the usual routines until the next crisis arrived.

And he'd be ready when it showed up. He only had one question.

Would the enemy be ready for him?

A LOOK AT: THE FAIRMONT MANEUVER

SCOTT STILETO BOOK 2

The Fairmont Maneuver is book two in the hard-edged, action thriller series – Scott Stiletto.

An urgent plea from a former flame brings CIA agent Scott Stiletto to San Francisco.

Ali Lewis was once a capable spy herself before striking out on her own, creating a fashion empire that stretches around the world. Now her father has been murdered, and Stiletto is the only man Ali can trust to learn the truth behind the killing.

Evidence points to a growing international conspiracy orchestrated by Iran involving the smuggling of nuclear bomb parts, kidnapped scientists, and a decades-old mafia-Silicon Valley alliance the government has been powerless to stop. And, somehow, Ali Lewis is caught in the middle.

Stiletto knows one thing for sure–this mission is personal.

For fans of Vince Flynn, Brad Thor and Don Pendleton.

AVAILABLE MAY 2019

ABOUT THE AUTHOR

A twenty-five year veteran of radio and television broadcasting, Brian Drake has spent his career in San Francisco where he's filled writing, producing, and reporting duties with stations such as KPIX-TV, KCBS, KQED, among many others. Currently carrying out sports and traffic reporting duties for Bloomberg 960, Brian Drake spends time between reports and carefully guarded morning and evening hours cranking out action/adventure tales. A love of reading when he was younger inspired him to create his own stories, and he sold his first short story, "The Desperate Minutes," to an obscure webzine when he was 25. Many more short story sales followed before he expanded to novels, entering the self-publishing field in 2010, and quickly building enough of a following to attract the attention of several publishers and other writing professionals.

Brian Drake lives in California with his wife and two cats, and when he's not writing he is usually blasting along the back roads in his Corvette with his wife telling him not to drive so fast, but the engine is so loud he usually can't hear her.